Twilight of Life...
Helpful Hints for Ageing Gracefully

Dr. Anil Gandhi

VISHWAKARMA PUBLICATIONS VP®

Twilight of Life... Helpful Hints for Ageing Gracefully

First Edition - October 2016
© Author

ISBN - 978-93-85665-34-9

The views expressed in this book are those of the author and do not necessarily represent the views of Vishwakarma Publications.

Published by:
Vishwakarma Publications
283, Budhwar Peth, Near City Post,
Pune- 411 002.
Phone No: (020) 20261157 / 24448989
Email: info@vpindia.co.in / Website: www.vpindia.co.in

Translated by
Dr. Anjali Patwardhan Kulkarni

English Edition Co-ordination
Translation Panacea

Cover
Abhishek Darekar

Typeset and Layout
Chaitali Nachnekar - Vishwakarma Publications

Dedication

Dedicated to all scientists, doctors, engineers, sculptors, poets and all those who have made exceptional contribution to their own field of work even after the age of sixty ...

Dedicated to all the Nobel Laureates who have rendered exemplary service to the cause of humanity...

Contents

Praise for the Book

Twilight is dusk, the period between day and night. This evening heralds the sunset of life, which is death and hence is very scary. Everyone is terrified of death. This fear is natural and innate. We are afraid of events likely to happen in the future, which is unknown to us. Hence, fear is an irrational feeling but we cannot deny its presence. Even the fear of old age is irrational but all the same, it exists and is real. If we wish to liberate ourselves from the fear of old age, we must gain all available knowledge about ageing. Dr. Gandhi, has done exactly this. He has given us all the possible information related to ageing. 'Old age' is not a disease. Medicines cannot cure it. Old age is a condition every one desires to reach. We need proper guidance regarding how one can spend one's old age happily and contentedly. We need to plan for old age beforehand. This planning should have health- related, financial, social, mental, psychological, cultural and spiritual facets. This book contains all the updated information based on scientific knowledge, which is presented in a very lucid style.

Dr. Anil Gandhi, deserves all applauds for writing this book. I feel that all people, young and old should read this book, contemplate and ponder about what it has to tell us.

Dr. H. V. Sardesai

Senior Physician and greatly admired Teacher of Medicine

Sincere congratulations to the author for such a perceptive, well-researched and studied discussion on the problems faced by the elders in our society.

The book beautifully depicts a society that has time to think about death that will inevitably arrive eventually and a people who are isolated because of the declining joint family system and a community, which is struggling to cope with the new technological changes.

It is proper to consider persons over the age of eighty as old.

The author not only depicts the problems faced by the aged but is also successful in suggesting a number of solutions. He has given useful tips to the elders regarding their body, mind and social presence.

Compliments to Dr. Anil Gandhi for discussing the need of old homes in a fast changing society and giving the readers copious information about institutions, which work for the old. I am convinced that this book is very useful not only for the old but for all those who are interested in social issues.

Dr. Kantilal Sancheti

Founder Director, Sancheti Orthopedic Institute, Pune

Twilight of Life... by Dr. Gandhi, is a book about ageing gracefully. Not only should the elders read it but the youngsters also should take heed. Each one of us is going to grow old. If all youngsters realize what it is to grow old, they would become more sensitive to the needs of the elders. The home will then become a haven with all the family members caring for each other. This book provides important information about government policies, schemes for the elderly, the rights of the old and the health care they require.

Kumar Ketkar

....

As Dr. Anil Gandhi is a medical practitioner, it is his prerogative to speak with authority on ageing. He has not confined his deliberations to the physical maladies of the aged alone but has considered the psychological, social, cultural, economic and administrative problems of the aged. He has also gone further and systematically discussed the solutions, which are available to us. This book is a testimony to the fact that Dr. Gandhi is an all rounder.

Shrikant Paranjpe
Director, Paranjpe Schemes, Pune

....

According to the predictions of a survey, the number of the aged is going to exceed that of the young in the coming century. Dr. Anil Gandhi's book Twilight of Life... Helpful Hints for Ageing Gracefully will prove to be an excellent guide for all senior citizens.

Old age is second childhood. In order to know how to spend this second childhood happily, everyone must read this book.

This book includes all the topics which are relevant to Ageing such as the physical and psychological needs of the old, their work out, illnesses, laws meant for protecting them, government policies and schemes, institutions meant for their support, old homes, and addresses of institutions which help the aged and also tips regarding precautions to be taken while seeking help.

Everyone must possess this excellent book.

Best wishes to all the senior citizens for Happy Ageing!

Rajeev Kulkarni
HelpAge India
94220220699

Foreword

Much is made of India's demographic dividend of an overwhelming proportion of youth in its population, but rarely do people talk or write about its senior citizens. This book by Dr. Anil Gandhi is departure from the usual and is filled with wisdom and understanding of the new paradigm of ageing. The elderly are a precious asset of the nation, being the repository of accumulated knowledge. Rich with experience they provide moorings to a society. Though India has not yet reached that stage, it is not yet far behind in becoming an 'aging population' with decreasing mortality, and, most importantly, declining fertility. By definition an elderly person or a 'Senior Citizen' is a person who is above the age of 60 years.

The experience of being older is also changing. Post-independence, the breakdown of the social fabric of the Indian families and the formation of an increased number of nuclear families coupled with longer life spans resulted in the aged population slowly getting side-lined and disadvantaged. The neglect of a large population of the country is loss of a considerable potential as well as a benefit of the future. This has been highlighted by Dr. Gandhi. It is also heartening to note that he has highlighted the role of civil society and also the pioneering work of HelpAge India across the country and the committed work of Janseva in Pune besides others.

Dr. Anil Gandhi in his book "Twilight of Life" deals with the life cycle of ageing, its joys and sorrows, its trials and tribulations. Every individual should read the book to understand the cycle and the decline of the body and its associated disabilities. The book focuses upon the need for all to realize the significance of 'ageing gracefully'. The recent developments in medical science have helped people to live longer lives but the most important concern is to live a longer, better and fulfilled life. Dr. Gandhi emphasizes on how one can achieve this quality of life through developing a positive attitude. In the twilight of life, the seniors face physical as well as mental turbulence. Ill health devastates their body and mind. With utmost respect to the thoughtfulness of man, we must think about the solutions to solve these problems. Ageing is also leading to the sublime where every soul is on a path of discovery and realisation. This path may be akin to "Vanaprastha" mentioned in our ancient texts but this path of soul searching may be an appropriate path in India as we all are brought up in a rich culture of spirituality. However the book has some very useful and practical tips on healthy ageing as well which are useful from a food and exercise regime to lead to active ageing.

I do hope the book will motivate and encourage others and elders to work towards active ageing and also inspire other organisations and the governments to do more for the senior citizens in the country.

Mathew Cherian
Chief Executive
HelpAge India
C-14 Qutub Institutional Area
New Delhi -110016

Preface

When life initially began on the earth, the first living organisms to be created were extremely minute ones. Later in the course of evolution, plants, animals and humans were born. Whether it is the smallest of creatures or a super intelligent human being, each living organism is driven by the natural instinct of living and propagating its species and possesses the necessary wisdom for it. They are able to prepare for difficulties such as inclement weather, water and food crisis beforehand and plan accordingly. The flora and fauna, insects, birds and beasts all prepare for the coming season so that they do not have to face scarcity of food and lack of shelter. The human being is more intellectually gifted than all the other living beings. Man alone can design long-term plans for dealing with natural or manmade calamities. Only man is able to predict the future disasters with the help of the wisdom he acquires from his experience. Man can think, develop ideas, worry and find solutions to ward off the agonizing issues and plan for measures, which can be useful in emergencies, only because of the advanced intelligence he possesses.

The other species take care of their young ones only until they become self-dependant after which their relationship ends. Man not only looks after his offspring for a long period but also cares for the elders in the family. Man caters to the elders' needs of food, clothing and shelter and health care.

The seniors have usually enjoyed a respectable position in the family. Their guidance was considered very useful. The elders had an important role to play in the rearing of the young ones. The house used to be contented with lots of people. With the change in times, this picture of a happy home has altered completely. The old can no longer depend upon the young for support and respect for elders is in short supply. The elders are doomed to spend the evening of their life in isolation, helplessness and despondency. Those whose financial condition is good, who are accompanied by their spouse usually have lesser problems as compared to those who have to stay alone. Those who have neither a partner nor loving company and whose young relatives are either unwilling to or unable to lend support have to live a very miserable life.

The younger generation witnesses this scenario and so they have already started preparing in advance for their old age that is quite far away. Since this awareness did not exist in the past or the elders were not financially strong now they have to live a wretched existence. It is the responsibility of the society and the younger generations to provide them facilities at least enable them to live respectably as human beings. Will the younger generation demonstrate this vision is the question?

In the twilight of life, the seniors face physical as well as mental turbulence. Ill health devastates their body and mind. With utmost respect to the thoughtfulness of man, we must think about the solutions to solve these problems. Man is on the higher rung in the evolutionary chain. These deliberations will certainly help the seniors to solve their problems but it will also help the youngsters to realize that they too will have to face all these maladies in their old age. This will help to fulfill altruistic as well as selfish goals.

Twilight is the period when the blistering sun sets and the cool moonlight is about to pervade the world. It is a period caught between day and night. Life also goes through similar stages. This is the period when one should end the feelings of self-indulgence, pride, envy and anger and try to derive peace and the calmness that comes with contentment. I have tried to discuss from a number of angles the various measures that will enable the elders to attain the desired gratification.

Prin. Dr. Anjali Patwardhan Kulkarni, has generously spared her valuable time for translating my book Ya Katarveli. Her choice of apt words and her great command on English language makes it an original book rather than a translation. I salute her for the exemplary work.

Shri Bharat Agarwal of Vishwakarma Publications have helped me from time to time in very many ways. I am indebted to them for having willingly agreed to publish the present book.

I am beholden for the generous words of praise for the book expressed by Dr H. V. Sardesai, Dr. K. H. Sancheti, Dr. Vinod Shah, Shri Shrikant Paranjpe of Athashri project and Shri Rajeev Kulkarni of HelpAge, India.

I am happy that I have been able to express my views on a relevant topic that was weighing on my mind for a very long time.

Thank you all!
Dr. Anil Gandhi

Translator's Note

I feel very fortunate that the work of translating, Twilight of Life... Helpful Hints for Ageing Gracefully came to me. I feel deeply connected with the book personally, because I am witness to all the ageing problems discussed here as my mother is just eighty-four years 'young' and I am on the verge of stepping into senior citizenship.

The book originally written in Marathi entitled, **'Ya Katerweli... Ananadi Wrudhatwakade Watchal,'** by Dr. Anil Gandhi discusses the problems faced by the aged and suggests solutions at a time when the Indian population is enjoying the benefits of enhanced longevity and bracing up to face the challenges arising out of longer lives. In the postmodern age of single families, 'selfies' and selfish interests, such a book that warns us against the self centeredness of the society is the need of the times. The book gives copious information about the problems faced by the aged, physical, psychological and financial maladies and offers solutions to them. The details about the various institutions such as Athashri, Janseva Foundation, HelpAge India and others offer alternatives of hassle- free living for the old.

Dr. Gandhi writes in a very simple, appealing and lucid style. He has been able to make a very serious topic like 'Ageing' very 'engAgeing' and there are sunny spots of lighthearted humor, which makes reading the book a pleasant experience.

His allusions to and quotations from Marathi literary works such as 'Natsamrat' and 'Dyaneshwari' speak for his literary acumen but were a real challenge to translate into English because of the culture specific expressions.

In the Marathi language we often use passive voice to express humility which usually does not read well in English expressions. It was indeed very interesting to translate Dr. Gandhi's modest Marathi diction.

Old age is very close to death and hence the lengthening of the shadows and the vanishing into the dark is but inevitable. It is inspiring to read how the author emphasizes the need for a positive attitude towards life and the will to live until life abides.

I am reminded of the English poet Dylan Thomas' poem, 'Do Not Go Gentle into That Good Night' in which invokes his father who is on death bed,

Do not go gentle into that good night,

Old age should burn and rave at close of day;

Rage, rage against the dying of the light.

The book elaborates Thomas's approach, which each one must have Twilight of Life!

Best wishes to all for ageing with grace!

Dr. Anjali Patwardhan Kulkarni
Principal,
Gokhale Education Society's
N.B.Mehta Science and Commerce College,
Bordi,Palghar

Some Heartfelt Thoughts

Dr. Anil Gandhi has written this book entitled Twilight of Life... with a sense of a social obligation towards the senior citizens and all the institutions, which work for the cause of the old. His commitment is evident on every page of the book.

Dr. Gandhi has very aptly described in this book, the turbulence that a person's mind and body goes through when she or he is in twilight of life. He has also suggested solutions to the problems of the aged, referred to the physical and mental exploitation of the aged, laws protecting the aged, economics related to the old and described in details the philanthropic work done by institutions such as HelpAge India, Janseva Foundation and others in a very lucid manner. Dr. Gandhi has gone further to spread the message of 'a contented mind' to make the period of old age a happy one. He has also commented on 'how to live in the present', and has lent a strong mental support to all the ageing parents around. I am reminded of an important thought expressed by the great thinker late Shivajirao Bhosle. At that moment, he was addressing the senior citizens at our Janseva Foundation's, home for the aged at Ambi. He said, "There is great joy in living life, and old age is the most fascinating stage of life. The setting sun appears so attractive and it showers gold upon the earth as it goes."

Dr. Gandhi does not look at the seniors from just an emotional point of view. While expressing satisfaction at the increasing number of seniors due to increased longevity he is also aware that this escalating number is going to create a big socioeconomic problem for the country. He speaks about the severity of the issue and suggests measures to counter it. In a way, Dr. Gandhi has alerted the society and the government about the probable predicament.

The senior citizens have a very important role to play in the development of the society. Their experience, their wisdom, the values they imbibe all this makes the society very strong in all respects. Every element in the society must pay serious attention to the problems faced by the aged and help to alleviate them. Both the generations should attempt to ensure that the young grandchildren remain attached to the home. This is indispensable if we wish to retain intergenerational solidarity.

Today the total population of the aged in India is twelve crore, out of which 15% are over the age of eighty and 25% of them are bedridden. The major part of the work for the aged takes place in the urban areas. Many of the aged people are members of one or the other organization for the old and hence organized but the 65% of the aged who live in the rural areas are unorganized. They face a lot of inconvenience as most of the facilities and schemes launched for the old by the central and state government do not reach the villages at all. Hence, the aged living in the rural areas have to face many hassles.

The major characteristic feature of the Indian culture, which is lauded all over the world, is the joint family system.

Unfortunately, threatened by Western ideology it has now weakened considerably and is on the verge of extinction. At the beginning of the twenty first century, a number of problems arose in the Indian family system itself. The joint family system is on the decline. One measure to counter this problem is to establish homes for the aged. Establishing such homes can never be our aim but it is a means to solve the predicament. This reminds of the thoughts expressed by the renowned scholar of saint literature Late Shri Balasaheb Bharde. He had said that," the family is the first center for the humans to render their services. The feelings one has for the family must be extended to make the whole world as one family." There are numerous institutions in our country as well as in the world, which are trying to promote the concept of the world as one family. Our Janseva Foundation also is like a step forward in that direction. I am extremely thankful to Dr. Gandhi for writing a detailed chapter on Janseva Foundation in this book.

I am greatly pleased with Dr. Gandhi. In spite of being an expert surgeon, he has a literary, lucid, simple and engaging style of writing. He has very aptly made use of rural and urban sayings and adages as well as inspirational thoughts from Sanskrit while dealing with such a serious a topic as 'Ageing'. This has made the whole matter in the book very convincing. Thus, the topic of 'Ageing' has reached the readers in the form of 'Conserving Age'. A number of old age institutions are functional all over Maharashtra. I am confident that this book will reach all of them and the senior citizens will make the best use of the book. The reception of this book will inspire Dr. Gandhi to write still further and I give him my best wishes for his future endeavor.

This book will be published in a special function to mark International Day of Older Persons, which is another reason for our elation.

Dr. Vinod Shah (MD)

Founder President
(Janseva Foundation, Pune –Special Advisor UNO
International Director, International Federation on Ageing
Mobile: 9823011760/ 020 24538787/8

The Spring of Life

The process of birth and blossom has continued eternally right from the origin of the earth and will go on until infinity. Strangely, though, the 'Intelligent Man' owing to his ignorance has decided that this life is transitory and perishable. When man realized that death was inevitable, prompted by fear, he imagined that the living being constitutes two aspects; one an immortal aspect called the soul and the second a perishable one called the body. The soul is everlasting and moves out of the body in which it resides just as one may change one's clothes. This further led to a commonly held firm belief in the idea about the rebirth of the soul. Thoughts and principles put forth by various religions reinforced this further. The strong wish to be able to persist for a considerably longer period with the same body one has received at birth, led to attempts of dodging and escaping death or discovering means to achieve perpetuity. The concept of 'Amrut' , 'elixir of life', originated out of this urge. It is not surprising to see how this led to the myths of churning the ocean from which 'Amrut' or nectar fell into Gods' hands .The Gods stole the urn holding the Amrut and tried to run away and so on. Further, when man started to research various chemicals, which could bring deathlessness to the human being, he was unsuccessful and did not find any.

Recent scientific studies have proved that whatever man has been searching for, so far actually resides within him. The union of male sperm and female ovum produces a new seed, which germinates into a new plant, grows and flourishes to reach the stage of fruition. The DNA, which is present in every living being, is the determining aspect, which continuously multiplies cells and sustains the life element relentlessly. It is perpetually alive and this can be considered as 'eternity'. The everlasting band of the DNA is transferred to the forthcoming new creation in the form of new cells, which means that the DNA is immortal, or at most expresses itself in a newer being. It is important to note that the transfer of DNA does not depend upon the account of virtues or sins committed in the previous births. Needless to say that every person should follow the rules of conduct and social behavior, necessary for living a life worthy of a human being. One may call it by any name, religion, ethics, abiding by the law, virtuosity but they are all important for safeguarding the intelligence and humanity of the human race.

While speaking about human beings, the origin of life- the fetus takes root in the mother's womb, rapidly develops and grows to a size, which looks like the bonsai of a fully-grown human being at birth. From the stage of germination to the stage of birth, the body gradually grows throughout life. However, the speed is comparatively lesser than during the fetus stage and a few years during childhood. As the youthful stage passes on into old age, the growth rate is negligible while on the contrary there is a considerable amount of loss. As the calculations move on from addition to subtraction, the individual grows into the physical and mental condition of an adult, senior individual and then an elderly person. It is now possible to understand these calculations due to the advances in Molecular Biology, Genetic Engineering, Chromosome Mapping and our ability to make changes in it. We can change our future to some extent with the help of recent developments made by scientists. It is now possible to take measures to ensure that hereditary sicknesses such as high blood pressure, heart disease, diabetes and albino do not occur at all. One can decide one's own destiny. Man has thereby started interfering with God's job of finalizing human fate. As a result, the belief that there is some superior power high up in the heavens who is the creator, preserver and destroyer of the universe no longer holds any credence. We have lost faith in the idea of God. The Centre no longer holds and things fall apart …

Research has found that cells in the human body split and recharge at least fifty to seventy times in one's lifetime. During each division, one base telomere pair of chromosomes gets reduced and when this happens for about sixty times the necessary telomere is no more and that causes the death of the cell. However, before this happens every cell has multiplied itself innumerable times and produced so many new cells that it has already ensured that it becomes immortal. The decrease in telomeres leads to the wearing of cells that in turn results in the exhaustion of the body. We usually describe this as' ageing of the body', or 'wear and tear of the body'. Because of this degeneration, the structural and functional body processes are likely to slacken. It has not been possible to suspend this process of degeneration completely but some amount of success is possible in slowing down this process.

There are two major aspects involved in the process of ageing. The first is the genetic aspect. Genetic engineering has been able to change this factor to a limited extent. However, the second aspect, which is nurturing or taking good care of one, is very much in our hands. In order to ensure positive effects, one must be careful regarding consuming a balanced diet, taking physical and mental exercises in the right proportion and ascertaining stress free mental peace. Various illnesses have a negative effect. If one is able to maintain one's immunity level, be able to take adequate preventive measures against diseases and get proper treatment for illnesses when they occur, it is possible to decelerate the speed of ageing.

Those who believe in God and who wish to lead a hassle free life, those who wish to avoid illnesses, consult soothsayers and astrologers with their horoscopes and conduct worships and yagnyas, observe fasts and take vows. This never helps in warding off the tribulations. It is necessary that proper medical investigations should be conducted with the help of advanced pathological (blood and urine) as well as imaging tests. Along with cleanliness and hygiene, regular exercises, balanced diet and mental peace it is also necessary to take the preventive vaccines in order to avoid any sickness. It is possible to delay ageing by curing diseases with the help of early diagnosis and treatment, or avoiding them by improving one's immune system. This will result in greater longevity. Merely benedictions given by religious gurus, pundits or our elders for a long life are not enough. However, many simple-minded people believe that such blessings will come true. They waste precious time, money and energy seeking good wishes. If we are careful, we will not need to do this. There is a lot of similarity between childhood and old age. 'Preserving the child in you' should not be the motto of just poets. In order that all share this maxim, everyone must revive and enjoy the memories of one's own childhood.

The science that studies ageing is known as Gerontology. The branch of study of the diseases caused by ageing is called Geriatric Medicine.

Thus, it is certainly possible to slower down the pace of ageing but we must remember that every cell faces its death due to the process of ageing. Even if cells die, they leave behind them their characteristics in the form of newborn cells. They are true to the adage, "In death do we live".

Evidence from the Puranas proves that death is the outcome of ageing but it is possible to be immortal. King Yayati tried to achieve immortality. He was not successful in his attempts but had he known about the deathlessness of the DNA cells he would have been happy to know that his wish would be fulfilled. He would not have had to beg people for exchanging his age with their youth.

We should all think carefully about how this journey, which begins from a small shoot of life, blossoms and reaches old age can become less problematic, more comfortable and a happy one.

From Generation to Generation

Life is made up of the good and the not so good. Nevertheless, we all wish that our lives should be free from the not so good things. We make a mountain out of a molehill of our sufferings while we hardly care for the other's problems. For instance, old age is one thing which none of us would like to face. If life does not end in premature death, each one of us is aware that old age is inevitable and yet we aspire to remain young. Mostly youngsters realize very late or refuse to accept the fact that even their old age is bound to arrive. It rarely happens that one learns from the mistakes of the elders or their careless attitude towards their health, which has been responsible for early ageing in their case. One can neither buy wisdom nor transfer it. However, if we keep our ears, eyes and nose open and be receptive we can learn a lot. It is necessary to follow the sincere and time-tested advice given by elders, avoid bad habits, and try to have a good diet, exercise well, achieve mental peace and strike a balance between work and relaxation. It may be difficult to manage all this in the competitive age of today but we can certainly make a conscious effort towards it.

There naturally exists a difference of opinions between any two generations. Their thoughts, food habits, apparel, sleeping routine, volume at which to hear music and so many other practices are bound to be different. It has already been said that, "just as the water in different ponds is bound to be different, the thoughts in different minds are going to be dissimilar." It is quite unlikely that everything that one individual or one generation follows is right. Every generation must keep this in mind. They must try to understand each other and avoid blaming the others. In this context one is reminded of the conversation between 'Bembtya' and his father at the end of P.L. Deshpande's play, "Asa mi Asami". It is quite evident that such dialogues between the old and the new generations will continue to be exchanged in the future too.

The joint family system followed in the Indian society in the past was undoubtedly a boon. It was lauded the world over. However, in our blind imitation of the Western culture the joint family system is slowly being swept away. We accepted the wrong changes. We have experienced the accelerated speed of these changes in the past fifty years.

Our parents reared us in our childhood; they gave us education, imbibed ethical values in our behavior, taught us good thoughts, searched for a suitable match for marriage, helped us to find means to make a living and made available rented or owned house to live in. Our parents used to provide us with all such facilities. Later, when our parents became aged, when old age made them frail, their sources of income had shrunk and they suffered ill health, became handicapped and dependant it was our duty to take care of them, fend for them, nurse them and lend them physical as well as mental support become their walking stick. This has been a characteristic feature of Indian culture and tradition.

At the same time, the wife would receive guidance as well as assistance from the mother while doing the daily household and kitchen chores. The father would share some words of wisdom with his son that would prove useful while facing the battle of life. These things were extremely invaluable. The grandchildren looked upon the grandparents as a very strong support. The grandparents doted on them and derived immense pleasure from their childish pranks and babbling talk. If the daughter in law was working, the grandparents contributed by looking after the children, by nurturing them with the right values and paying attention to their studies. This was the picture of an ideal joint family. Alas… Our blind imitation of the Western culture, the pressures of reality or the changed course of the stream of life, all these and more could be responsible for the collapse of the joint family system. We must say that, some evil eye cursed the happily functioning joint family system and now it has almost become extinct. People became increasingly self-centered and self-interest consumed their entire existence. Folks were at logger heads, the age of the equation of "we are two, ours will be one or two," dawned and the elders became unwanted members in the family. They also considered that the health issues of the aged were as a bother. The soaring expenses which had to be made especially for the old people became burdensome. Their suggestions became a sort of constant nagging. This led to the breakdown of the undivided family. The younger generation lost their protective chaperon while the older generation felt that the very ground on which they were firmly anchored was giving way. Children were less pampered while the elders lost their most valued grandchildren. Everyone suffered because of the loss of the joint family system. Everyone was a loser in this game.

Today's youth fail to realize that the problems, which riddle the lives of senior citizens today, are also going to torment them in the future. It is quite likely that the tribulations in store for them may be graver ones. They seem not to learn anything from the mistakes made by the seniors. The situation until now is quite bearable. However, when one sees how the youngsters do not hesitate even to drive away the old from their own homes, or abuse them, one feels extremely dejected. There are cases one reads in the newspapers or watches on the television about children aged eight or ten, threatening their grandparents for not giving them enough pocket money or even stabbing them with a knife. Such incidents are heart rending and disturb us. We can hardly do anything about it and simply turn the other way saying, "What cannot be cured has to be endured."

There is a tremendous increase in life expectancy owing to the brilliant progress made by medical science and the increased amount of health care awareness among people. The upper age limit has improved by almost thirty years since our independence. This increase in life expectancy can be seen not only in our country and society but also all over the world. This is the brighter side of the local as well as global situation. Nevertheless, when problems faced by individuals start increasing they also become global and escalate into becoming a universal malady. Discussions on this topic are held on a universal level. It is the need of the hour to find out solutions and apply them on a global scale. Today this problem has augmented in size but in the next thirty or forty years it will grow to an unmanageable global degree. Hence, it is the need of the hour to find out a solution for this problem on not only the individual level but also on the social, national and universal plane. We must take heed before the predicament magnifies into a crisis. All families, social service groups and governments of all nations should proactively participate in the drive to uproot this problem.

Numerous studies are conducted on the statistical data of the increase in the number of senior citizens. For example, this is the scenario in The United States of America:

In 2013, the number of citizens above the age of sixty-five was 44.7 million (14.1%). The estimated population in 2060 is going to be 98 million (21.7%).

The statistical figures for India are different. At present, the number of youth is larger but with advancement in time, the then population will have a majority of senior citizens. The percentage of elders above the age of sixty-five is going to be 5.3% while the percentage of children below the age of fourteen will be 31.2%. After about thirty to thirty five years the percentage of old people will be 35-40%. Taking this into consideration we are required to address the problem of ageing and find solutions to it on an urgent basis.

Transformation in Body and Mind

As one grows up gradual changes take place in the body as well as mind. This reminds of a verse from the play, Sangit Sharada, that goes like this,

"Not so old you know, just three quarters of a century

Yet too young for marriage,

With some silver in his hair,

A clean baldhead,

Yet not so old you know, just one quarter less for a century."

As age advances, major or minor changes are bound to occur in all the organs of the body. The manifestation of these changes could be different in different individuals and different genders. Grey hairs, hair fall, balding are some of the changes observed. It seems that currently both these changes have become eager to manifest themselves, because one observes these changes happening to people before their time. The evident changes are dry, freckled, wrinkled skin, loose and sagging skin under the neck, fat deposits along the waist area leading to a potbelly especially in men, while in women there is an apparent change in the walking style. Because of wear and tear of the knees, their gait changes from that of a swan to a duck. Their proportionate figure becomes imbalanced on account of fat deposits on the belly region causing 'tyres' as well as on the underarms, hands and thighs and loose, sagging breasts. The sparkle in the eyes is dimmed; spectacles accompany one's forties because the eyes lose their capacity of accommodation. This is followed by cataract and glaucoma leading to loss of eyesight. The ears refuse to hear. Since one cannot hear properly, one depends on guesswork leading to a lot of misunderstanding and confusion or then one may take resort of hearing aids. The sense of smell also diminishes slowly. The ear lobes start to dangle. There is sufficient dental health care awareness among people and owing to the advancement in dentistry, very few people are required to use dentures these days. Hence, shrunken cheeks have become a rare sight.

The large amount of calcium loss leads to brittle, painful bones, which are likely to fracture easily. This condition is more rampant in women. The wearing of joints leading to joint pain and the consequent joint replacement is more frequently seen in the case of women than in men. So it becomes necessary to build their homes in sunlight. If one exposes oneself to the early morning sunrays for about thirty to forty minutes it helps to transform the cholesterol in the blood into vitamin D. This is doubly beneficial as it reduces cholesterol in the blood and exempts one from consuming vitamin D tablets. The calcium in the bones reduces rapidly, in women after menopause. They should consume milk, bananas and calcium supplements to avoid problems arising out of calcium deficiency.

Advancing age also causes reduction in the rate of metabolism. Hence, it is necessary to bring about changes in diet as well as lessen the intake. Constipation is on the rise and in order to avoid it, one must consume green leafy vegetables (not soups), tubers such as carrot, radish, beetroot and fruits in a larger quantity. Ageing also causes reduction in hormonal levels leading to decrease in sex drive. Dryness in the genital tract causes discomfort and can be reduced by applying lubricants when necessary. It is therefore advisable to lessen sexual behavior and accept the moderate measure in which one can successfully enjoy it.

One should reduce intense physical activity as the muscles become weak in old age but a continuous exercise regime will prove helpful in maintaining muscle strength. Deep breathing, pranayam, yogasana help in retaining the flexibility of the body for a longer period. This helps in reducing the possibility of physical injuries. Since exercise helps in maintaining the power of the lungs, diseases related to the respiratory tract are less troublesome. As age advances the possibility of decorations such as anemia, hypertension, diabetes is on the rise. Once these ornaments adorn your body it is very difficult to cast them away. Due to the thickening, narrowing and hardening of the blood vessels owing to blood pressure, diabetes blood supply to vital organs such as the heart, lungs, kidneys, brain gets reduced. This leads to life threatening maladies such as heart disease and paralysis. Consumption of tobacco is a booster for all these diseases. All forms of nicotine intake should be strictly avoided. Enlargement of the prostate glands in elderly men, is the cause of frequent urination, especially during the night. They often suffer from problems such as urine infection and urine retention. Women too suffer because of the narrowing of the passage post-menopause. Both men and women should seek the physician's advice and treatment for these matters.

If their sexual life continues, men are likely to suffer less from prostate cancer. If sexual relations in both men and women are harmonious, that leads to increased contentment and mutual concern. A happy mind helps to increase the body's immunity. Let the mind be contented!

When women breastfeed their children they are overjoyed that they can lactate. It helps to increase their power of resistance and almost insulates them from the possibility of breast cancer. Breast-feeding has its own advantages.

Cancer is the ace enemy of human kind. It is likely to occur in any part of the body except the hair. In old age, women are more likely to suffer from cancer of the breast and ovary while men suffer from prostate cancer. Considering this possibility, it is advisable to get oneself thoroughly checked by a good physician. The blood supply to the brain is reduced and the brain does not remain alert to new learning due to blood pressure and diabetes. The capacity to forget exceeds the capacity to remember. In such an eventuality, old people go on repeating things that they have already spoken. When forgetfulness crosses a certain limit it, turns into a disease called 'dementia'. 'Alzheimer' is the gravest form of forgetfulness. 'Parkinson' is another troublesome malady and a small blood clot or bleeding leads to the awfully challenging and debilitating disease like an attack of 'Paralysis'. If we wish to avoid these diseases related to the brain, we need to exercise the mind and the body regularly, avoid any addictions and adopt a life style that will help to control blood pressure, diabetes and stress. In cases where diseases cannot be avoided it is better to treat them with the advice from a proper doctor. Nevertheless, it is always wiser to prevent them rather than cure them.

In spite of adopting preventive measures such as physical and mental exercise, a healthy diet, adequate sleep if one falls ill it is always prudent to take the necessary treatment without wasting any time. One must follow the doctor's advice regarding which pathological tests to undergo, how frequently for e.g. diabetes and blood pressure.

In case the elders are incapable of visiting the doctor the youngsters in house like the son or daughter-in-law or grandchildren should take the responsibility. In the good old days of Ramayan we are told that dutiful sons like Shrawan would take even the blind parents on a pilgrimage so that they would accumulate 'punya', good deeds. The children of today should take their parents to the doctor, which is a means of accumulating good deeds like taking them on a pilgrimage. If there are no children or if they are staying far away abroad, relatives and friends or social service institutions have to take up this responsibility.

Those who need to be served are called 'service takers' while those individuals and institutions which render such service are called, 'service providers or givers'. In some developed nations, even the government offers such services. One expects that as far as possible the elders must avoid taking such assistance but the service providers also must render their services when need be in a pleasant manner.

If the elders realize and accept the fact that their physical and mental capacities will wane as time goes by, occasions for the need for the give and take of services will be considerably reduced.

So far, we have discussed the various physical and mental maladies along with the infirmity caused to the brain and the measures to treat them. One more aspect, that of psychological sickness is also very important. Usually we pay more attention to the physical problems and do not take psychological conditions very seriously. Now the relatives, institutions, government all are waking up to the gravity of the psychological problems of the old. This is good news for such patients provided they understand it.

Happy Old Age

It is a usual practice to decide youth or old age based on physical age. The infant is quite naive but as it grows it likes to imitate the elders in the family .The girl child plays the role of mother while the boy that of the father. While imitating them and their grandparents they don the grandfather's cap, glasses and hold the walking stick and also try to fit into the oversize shoes. With the passing of time, these games and grandpa's clothes vanish from the children's lives. But the wish to behave like grownups or grow up fast continues to be with the youngsters. Youth is a period when wishes, aspirations, thoughts and actions ride at a fast pace. Nevertheless, once the person retires from service or business this mental setup takes a beating. The emptiness, which suddenly pervades life, becomes unbearable. One feels tortured by the seemingly reduced importance in the family. One becomes anxious about one's future.

The main reason for this mental disquiet is that the rules for age of retirement have not changed with the increased rate of life expectancy. This means that old age is not a physical age but a mental stage. Even the people who are physically and mentally strong, after crossing the age of sixty, refuse to accept that they are old. They wish to enjoy life fully. On the contrary, the mentally weak people are likely to be physically fragile too.

Today even people aged between sixty and seventy-nine feel that they are yet quite young.

Still in the Prime of One's Youth !

They say that the twenty first century is the age of advanced technology. Medical science has progressed at almost missile speed and has transformed human life entirely. The average life span of humans has also increased considerably. This extended longevity is both a boon as well as a bane of the twenty first century. The unprecedented speed with which life is prolonged and the considerable drop in birth rate has led to reduction of the number of productive young people and increase in the number of elders. This situation has disturbed the financial equation internationally. Not only the common person but also the media and the politicians responsible for determining the national policies are paying attention to this problem that they realize is a very grave one.

A hundred years ago, a person turning sixty would be considered a rarity and would be greatly appreciated. The usual picture of an old person would not be complete without a bare mouth, a baldhead where no hair could grow and a bent bowed back .Retiring from the job meant becoming useless. He was supposed to chant God's name and in anticipation of his call. This picture has completely changed in the twenty first century. Now it is quite usual that even at the age of eighty, the teeth are intact, the brain is active and the body is standing straight. The definition of age has changed. People in the age group of sixty to seventy- nine can be considered as middle aged and only those above eighty can be termed as old or senior. Initially it was in the developed nations that these definitions changed but they are now applicable to even the developing and under developed countries. In this context, I cannot resist narrating an experience I had in a London hospital, where I was working in the year 1974.During those days we Indians believed that with the onset of the sixties one became senile and depended on the walking stick for support. One was supposed to just wait for the end to come. In Saint Marks' Hospital as I was recording the history of a patient I asked him in my routine manner, "How old are you?"

The surprised patient looked around and then at me. He asked me a counter question."Am I old?"

I was startled. I gathered myself and asked another question," Okay, How young are you?"

He replied, "That is the right question. I am just sixty- five".

This is how I faced an embarrassing situation in London in 1974.

Now even in India it is not very relevant to ask children, women and people up to the age of seventy-nine the question-- how old are you? Saying something like, "It is true that you are yet very young but could you tell your exact age?" could be the proper wording of the question.

Even in our country, this new category of senior citizens is increasing at a fast rate. However, for most of them their means of income stops at sixty years or is very meager. The younger generation is running its own rat race and hardly has any time or money to pay attention to the older members. While the present day seniors reared their children, they also respected, and cared for their elders. Not only in India but also all over the world, it is no longer possible for middle aged people (between 60and 79) according to the new definition, or the elders above eighty to depend upon their children for support. Hence it has become essential for the seniors to review and plan their financial needs, illness and social life anew. But this is possible only in the case of elders who belong to the higher middle class income groups. In an agricultural country like India where sixty percent of the population lives in the rural areas and has to work day in and day out to satisfy even the basic needs of life planning for future needs is indeed a luxury which they cannot afford. The poor, down trodden, backward in the rural areas face even more serious issues. The younger generation from among these can hardly manage to make both ends meet or they are likely to have migrated from their village to some city. But they are unable to take the responsibility of the elders because of their meager income, insufficient space to live and also their changed attitude. In such circumstances, the condition of the elders becomes very miserable. While they are unable to satisfy the basic needs of food, shelter, clothing and health they can hardly expect to lead a respectable life. Even mere living becomes an impossible thing. They suffer mutely, in a panic ridden condition unsure of being able to survive until even the next day. One hopes that if the following day fails to dawn in their lives it is a respite from the endless sufferings one has to endure. Negative thoughts like, 'death is the only relief' frequently arise but one keeps on enduring the injustice in life because death does not come so easily.

We must all realize that even the frail and physically challenged senior citizens have a right to lead a normal life. The affluent citizens who can afford to help in gratifying the needs of the under privileged elders must contribute on humanitarian grounds and carry out their social duties and responsibilities. Governments all over the world should build old homes, provide health care services, health insurance schemes, pension schemes and satisfy security related needs of the elders. The Governments should implement these schemes even if it would need to levy Social Security Tax on the wealthy people. It is their prime responsibility.

In the past few decades, Indian Government has implemented 'Indira Gandhi Wrudh Pension Yojana',' Rajeev Gandhi Jeevendayi Yojna' for health related issues. The senior citizens get some concession in travel fare and income tax also.

The percentage of illiteracy among elders in the rural areas is 70%.Even in the cities educated people who are physically or mentally ill hardly know about the government schemes meant for them. Either they are not aware of their rights or they do not have the mental and physical strength or capacity to fight for them. Neither is the governmental machinery bothered about the senior citizens nor are the politicians interested. Since their only aim is to satisfy their selfish benefits, they hardly care about their duties. As a result very few senior citizens can avail the benefits offered by the Government. Nothing good or bad is permanent .So why should we not hope that this corruption and apathy rampant in our system shall change one day for the better and the elders will comfortably be given the benefits they deserve?'When wishes are horses even beggars can ride'!

Considering the increase in life span, the elders should avoid depending on the younger generation for financial support. One must properly plan for one's own and spouse's future. Like the hero of the popular Marathi play, 'Natsamrat' or Shakespeare's renowned English play 'King Lear' one should not give away everything to the children. The house should go to the children after both the elders; man and wife are no more. One should properly plan the savings and deposits in the bank. If the nectar pots are all exhausted how will the bees come near them? If one intends to stay in a joint family one should not dominate the family members and also humbly refuse to be dictated by others. One should not impose one's views on others or be intolerant. It is also not good to harp upon one's ill health and keep nagging about it. One must occasionally give gifts to the younger family members and also volunteer to help in case financial difficulties. Advice should be given only when it is sought for and help rendered in the small daily chores.

It is difficult to learn new things in old age. The brain's capacity to accept new things is weakened in old age. However, old age brings in a lot of free time. One must try to gain knowledge of the available applications of new technology such as smart phones and internet and use it for one's purpose. One should also consult the physician on time to treat the physical and mental maladies that arise from time to time. One should also consider the lowering capability of the body and the mind and undertake exercises regularly. Doing one's chores independently by oneself helps in boosting confidence and creates joy.

These measures will help both the generations live together happily. In case it is not possible to stay together, they should live in separate households. They can help each other when need arises. If even this is not possible they can exercise the options of Athashri, Homes for the Aged or similar extended family facilities.

If we wish to lead our old age happily in peace and tranquility, we must adopt the mantra, 'live without expectations'.

The Love of Co-existence

What does 'love' mean exactly? Love is not just the prerogative of the humans alone. Even plants and birds make love. It is because of man's innate intelligence that the humans, like the multi coloured rainbow, can manifest numerous shades of love. We know about the mother's affection for her child. History, which tells us about how. When the doors of the fort were closed, Hirkani dared to jump across the ramparts of the fort to rush home to feed her hungry child, can never become obsolete. Anecdotes about the youthful Laila-Majnu, Heer –Ranjha have become immortal. Usually love between a young boy and a girl ultimately conclude in marriage. Experience has proved that even in arranged marriages, solemnized by the consent of the elders, which is a characteristic feature of Indian culture, love takes firm root and thrives between them through proximity. The reasons for the origin of the feeling of love may be different in different people and relations; nevertheless, love is after all love! It undoubtedly pleasures the brain.

It is said that 'God thirsts for devotion.' However, God is not an individual; God is a concept or a universal power. Therefore, it may not be too precise to state that God craves for love but it is an undeniable fact that man's brain certainly yearns for love. Man's life blooms due to love, is enriched and leads to satisfaction. During childhood, one enjoys the affection of the parents and siblings. In young age, the lover and the beloved enjoy the ecstasy of love. Post-marriage, their togetherness transforms their relationship like a well-seasoned pickle. As the association continues, the relationship matures still further. Even if the erotic aspect of this relationship lessens considerably, yet the two people have already become one existence. Mutual understanding and sacrifice replace the physical aspect of the relationship.

During young age, the bond between the husband and wife is very alluring and adoring. It also augments the ability to make sacrifices. The two cannot live without one another and they feel that they are inseparable. However, if confronted by the possibility of death each one would prefer to save oneself. This is termed as the prime need of evolution. One is reminded of the story one reads in Birbal and Badshah about the mother monkey and her child who are placed in a tank in which water is gradually filled. The mother finally, gets ready to sacrifice her child to save her own life. The story is apt and educative. However, it is also true that after saving oneself the first thing one remembers is one's beloved. This is true not only in the days of youth but also in the twilight of advanced age.

When the elders lose their ties with the family, the husband and wife are eager to support each other. They share their sorrow arising out of their estrangement from children and also when children turn them out of their house. They share the distress of severed relations or of being duped out of their land and property. Elders with words such as, 'May you stay eternally married', bless the bride during her marriage. This is because she must never have to face the life of a widow. I have not heard anyone blessing the bridegroom in this manner, ever. I have failed to understand this discrimination. In fact,

I feel it would be so nice if both died together so that no one will be left alone. In the past, the practice of Sati must have spared the girl the sorrow of loneliness. Nevertheless, even this was one sided. Burning a woman alive was inhuman and by abolishing the practice, religion was not tarnished, nor did it incur the wrath of the Almighty and invite the deluge! In short, it is important for both the partners that the silken bond of marriage remains strong and intact.

The death of a partner creates dismay and dejection. It happens in all ages. The problems, which arise after the death of a partner in young age and those, which arise in old age may be different. Comparatively it is easy to find a new partner, establish a live-in relationship or remarry in young age. The family and the society easily accept it as well.

Recently an old man of ninety posted his wish to remarry on Face book. There were many comments made on the post such as,' does he want a nurse in the form of a wife to take care of him? He should appoint a paid nurse instead. Or else go to a home for the aged and enjoy all the available facilities there'. It is wrong to presume that the sole objective of marriage is sexual gratification alone. It is a means of getting someone who participates in one's whole life. If this is true then it should not be decided on the condition of age. Can there be any hesitation in welcoming either the bonds of marriage or those of a live-in relationship if that means mutual sharing of joys and sorrows, establishing a dialogue and helping each other in times of need? Undoubtedly no! If it is a marriage, it will have to be followed by registration, rules and regulations.

If the man is wealthy and aged and if in such a marriage, the bride is economically weak she shall continue to legally enjoy financial benefits as the widow of that man. Is there anything wrong about it? But the old man's descendants may object to any such arrangement. If the old man has made wealth out of his own efforts the court supports the widow's right to that property as mentioned in the old man's will. Currently the partner's or the progeny's right to the deceased person's property even in a live-in relationship has received legal approval.

While discussing the twilight of life let us consider the love related requirements of the elders. Whether a love marriage or an arranged one, the initial days after marriage are full of dreams and excitement. The two are ready to sacrifice one's life for the other. The sky is the limit for them. After some time the realization of hard, harsh reality dawns upon them. The problems faced in everyday life gradually become evident to them. So far, they were attracted towards each other's beauty and virtues. Now the multi colored lens through which life appeared so attractive is removed from their eyes. They now start noticing the unattractive aspects of their partner. These facets become increasingly obvious to them. Initially the complaints are subdued but as days pass, they become evident to others also. Conflicts create a lot of noise and confusion. If both of them handle this phase with patience and maturity, this phase passes after a few days. Maturity brings in mellowness and thoughtfulness. One starts considering the fact that no one is perfect. Everyone has a weakness. It is now that the true phase of togetherness begins. Those couples who have lived together for many years develop the art of guessing the feelings in each other's mind even when they do not speak a single word, merely with the help of just body language and gestures. When they read these unsaid thoughts and do things for each other that is truly, matured love. With the decline of the joint family system, this kind of togetherness, constant company of one another has become very essential. No matter how much they love each other, in the eventuality of the death of one of the partners the loneliness in store for the other is distressing. If the man passes away first, comparatively the woman is more equipped to face the situation. Even though she is more emotional, by nature she is better prepared to face stress and tension and survive in unfavorable conditions. The household tasks she attends to, the kitchen work are her forte as she has performed them all her life. However, contrary to this if the man is left alone he cannot manage maintaining the house, cleaning the vessels and clothes because he is not used to doing these tasks. He cannot cook food. So a man left alone after the death of his wife becomes a very miserable person. However, the passing away of one's spouse leads to loneliness. There is no one to share one's misery and grief, no shoulder on which to rest one's head and weep and express sorrow. The home starts appearing like a big cellular jail and the lonely person feels like a prisoner sentenced to life imprisonment. In such circumstances when there is no one to share one's feelings with or be soothed one can consider keeping pets. They can fill in the vacuum created by the spouse's death to some extent. When one keeps a cat or a dog as a pet it is presupposed that, one takes good care of the pets' needs. If the person feeds and gives shelter to the pet, the pet will never desert her or him. The pets love the master. If you speak in their language, they listen to you without grumbling. They are disturbed when your eyes fill with tears. Dogs protect you from the other's harassment and even sacrifice their lives for the sake of their masters. No animal is as faithful as a dog, least of all the human being. Even if you may feed the humans, give them a handsome salary there is no guarantee that she or he will not run away with your valuables or cheat you for your property. So many senior citizens trust and love dogs more than they love and trust humans. Many old people the world over have bequeathed their property worth millions in their will, to their pets.

While keeping pets and enjoying their affection it is necessary to take care that one does not harm their young ones, or over step their fondness. If this happens, they will never forgive us. You reap what you sow If you give love you get love in return. Live and let live, that should be the motto.

Some people obtain love in the company of people but they also derive love from animals. This is not as part of the brain's needs. It is because they are animal friends or bird friends and wish to do something different from what others do. They establish a friendly bond with birds like the parrot, pigeon, peacock and harmless animals like the rabbit, tortoise or deer. Some others who wish to exhibit their adventurous side befriend animals like the elephant, tiger and lion as a hobby and care for them.

Dr.Purnapatre, from Chalisgaon, in spite of his time consuming medical practice, found time to develop his hobby of keeping a tiger as a pet. The tiger would move about freely around his bungalow. Even Dr. Praksah Amte along with his medical practice has developed a sanctuary for wild animals at Hemalkasa. He is very fond of his tiger, lion and snakes and even has an alligator as a pet. However, such hobbies are extremely expensive. If the wild animals are hungry, they can be dangerous.

Everyone has the right to be loved but we must be aware of the dangers of love for animals and beware of them.

Old people who are not respected in their families have to decide to live apart. The size of these people's homes should be just enough to satisfy their needs. In view of their health problems, they must avoid climbing staircases. An apartment that has the facility of an elevator is very advantageous. There should be a gym for exercising, a swimming tank, and a temple for the devout, which gives them mental peace and fosters positivity. They can also avail of common facilities such as maintenance and security. It is also possible to pass time chit chatting with the neighbors or seek help from them in times of emergency. Of course, this will be possible only if the help is mutual. However, in self-centered societies such as Mumbai they do not even know who stays next door. Such localities are not congenial for senior citizens. Specific arrangements should be made where senior citizens reside. There must be rods fitted in bathrooms for them to hold. Western style toilets are better than the Indian counter parts for painful knees. If a senior citizen slips on wet floors and falls down or suffers from problems related to the heart or an attack of paralysis, it is difficult for them to get up. So it is safe not to bolt the toilet and bathroom doors in case it is bolted there must be a small opening through which the bolt can be opened from outside. This will avoid the need to break open the door in times of an emergency. There should not be floor level differences in the house.

In those places where such apartments are not available or affordable, they can consider taking such apartments on rent. Those seniors who have not been able to make the necessary arrangements beforehand are compelled to take up any kind of residence and put up with all the disadvantages either along with the spouse or singly. The woman in Indian culture is a homemaker by default, she cooks and she works to earn. Therefore, even if she stays alone she does not face many problems regarding routine chores. Nevertheless, if a man has to stay alone he has to manage household work, clean the house and wash the clothes and the utensils, jobs which he has never had to do earlier. He cannot manage cooking food. So he has to depend upon food bought from outside. All the same, whether it is a woman or a man, lonesomeness is heart wrenching. Even if one does not miss sharing work, one certainly misses a partner with whom to share thoughts and feelings and obtain emotional as well as physical support in times of need. Nevertheless, one has to resign to one's fate and accept what is in store.

Movies such as Raja Paranjpe's 'Uun Paus'(1957-58) in Marathi and the Hindi movie 'Baagban' really touch the heart. Both the movies present the devastating picture of how those very children whom you have reared and nurtured all your life, educated them, taught them values, sacrificed your dreams for gratifying their wants, given your all for helping them grow, now turn away from you when you are old and need them so intensely.

In spite of knowing that their parents have retired, their economic condition is quite weak, they suffer from various health- related problems and that they are petrified yet many children separate the two and take responsibility of just one parent at a time. They treat them like waifs. The film 'Baagban' portrays this reality. When one of the partners falls sick the other has to make sneak phone calls. In spite of knowing that the medicines would not be available one suggests remedies while the other assures that the medicine is being taken regularly when actually there is no medicine at hand. Such scenes that depict the helplessness of both as well as the concern for one another certainly bring tears to the eyes.

Until recently, the number of divorces in India was comparatively less. At present, we are imitating the West and are increasing the number considerably. Earlier one felt that it was better to seek a divorce at an early age if one found out that the other partner was incompatible. Now divorces occur even at the ripe age of sixty. The number of men is greater but women are not far behind. These women feel that they have tolerated a lot for the sake of their children but now after the children are independent they no longer can stand their husband's injustice. Like-minded women formed associations of their own .These groups are helpful because the women listen to, share each other's problems, and make suggestions. Hail Women Power! Hail Women Empowerment!

Senior citizens' remarriages or live- in relations are a solution to some of the problems. One can consider the possibility of combinations of two women or two men or a man and a woman staying together. Many a times the next generation in the family does not approve of a remarriage even if the couple is going to stay apart from them. It also involves problems such as: if the marriage fails, it will create property disputes, alimony issues, legal hassles and endless trips to the court, which one cannot withstand. Hence it is convenient to stay with a same sex or different sex partner. In such circumstances establishments such as 'Athashri' or old age homes are more convenient. You will find details about 'Athashri' which is an extended residence for the aged, in the subsequent chapter.

The Mind That Is Ours!

The very thought of the human mind brings to our mind the unforgettable lines by the Marathi poet who was the possessor of unparalleled imaginative prowess, Bahinabai. She has described the human mind as an animal which how many ever times is turned away from a field full with crops returns repeatedly to feed on it. It is surprising to see how in certain occasions the human mind is as hard as a rock while in other instances it is even softer than a Shirish flower. As age advances, the human mind grows fonder and yielding. Even a casual comment or a slight change in someone's behavior is enough to hurt it. Especially when one's own child who has been the apple of the eye, on whom one showered all the affection possible, for building whose future one has sacrificed everything, if that same child uses words or actions which inflict wounds, it devastates the mind. It is difficult to console them. Even a deep wound made to the body, something as painful as a heart surgery can heal easily but not so with the invisible lesions caused to the mind, which make deep gashes. When in old age, when one expects to hear a few sweet words or be treated amicably by one's children, if it does not happen the disappointment is beyond endurance. In such circumstances, one has to surrender to the situation and treat the wound at least overtly. It is indeed better to follow the principle of resignation, 'What cannot be cured has to be endured'.

The seniors are more upset not with social neglect, physical or economic problems but are intensely tortured when connived at by their own people. The members of the younger generation have their own tribulations, their own compulsions or a lessening in their feelings for the elders, which makes them ignore the sacrifices, their loving parents made for them in the past. The elders must give up their increased insistence on things with advancing age. One must learn to avoid giving unasked-for-suggestions, interfering in the private matters of one's son and daughter in law, criticizing their behavior, passing nasty comments on the generation gap and also sharing them with outsiders. It is the duty of the seniors to appreciate the younger generation whenever they deserve to be complimented, help them in routine household work, look after the grand children and their lessons and participate in the family matters. In short, both the generations must agree that both are likely to make mistakes and should live together with understanding and tranquility. The mother in law should not be an obsessive suggestion maker and the daughter in law should not be completely allergic to suggestions made. In the past, the daughter in law would happily give up her parental home and consider her husband's home as her own. It is quite beneficial for both the parties when the two generations dwell together peacefully. But if this co-existence is not possible either because the new generation has gone to another place or even abroad for making a living then it is advisable to visit one another and help them in times of need and support them during economic and emotional hardships. We can witness a number of such examples around us. Distance can help to avoid differences arising in day-to-day affairs but can be helpful in rendering all kinds of help required in any emergency. An example of such help is found when usually these days the mother and the mother in law takes turns to assist the daughter or daughter in law residing in a foreign country, during her pregnancy, child birth and in the initial stages of post child birth care. At all other times it could be like 'the grass is greener on the other side of the mountain.' The NRI generation residing abroad can easily afford to render financial aid. They can also give emotional and economic support in the eventuality of serious illnesses. This is an ideal way of avoiding familiarity breeding contempt. The arrangement of staying apart but helping each other in times of need can also be considered as a contemporary edition of the joint family system. Some call it the Extended Family System.

The Changing Mentality

As a person advances in age, his mind, body and wealth all undergo a change. As children grow up the doting aspect is replaced by the need to discipline the child. Parents continue to pamper children in food related aspects but are strict when it comes to studies, exercise and inculcating good habits. They may often scold them and even administer corporal punishment to the children. After a certain age, even the children realize that all that their parents do is for their betterment. At a later stage, they become conscious of the 'self' and start considering themselves as smarter than their elders. They begin to tell lies and even back answer their parents. This feeling is on the rise once they get a job or start a business and begin to earn money. The respect for elders is on the decline. Then with marriage comes an adoring wife. In just the next few days one starts believing her complaints against one's parents. The fondness one has from childhood for one's parents is gradually on the decline. The domestic conflicts begin. With the coming of children one starts adoring them but the parents who are slipping into old age become burdensome. Small skirmishes turn into a battle. All this ends in the driving out the parents from their own or their children's house.

Just as the young undergo a psychological change, even the elders go through a similar phase of transformation. They cannot bear to hear their children whom they pampered and sacrificed everything for them, speak ill about them. The elderly couple discusses the reasons for such a transformation in the children. For various reasons this mental torture increases by the day. The feeling that they have become strangers in their own home is very disturbing. It leads progressively to stages of irritation, anger, helplessness and dejection finally leading to devious, measures and scheming or ends in the home for the aged.

The young are engrossed in competing, doing overtime at their job or business, following etiquettes, even managing corruption in order to pile up money for the future or buy a house of their own. The parents who slogged to make all the facilities available to the child start losing their confidence when they enter the last stage of their life. Yet the society respects them. They mix with people; they are cordially invited to attend weddings and other functions. Whatever the reasons one feels honored by the relatives, friends, colleagues in the office, and the society. Gradually they inevitably reach the rung of retirement. Since one has reached sixties the body and mind, both are tired. The enthusiastic stages are left far behind. Resting for some time feels good but as income reduces, one has to be thrifty. One has to think twice about the necessity of buying anything, ensure that it is moderately priced to cut down on expenses. Since the nectar in the form of money is limited, bees in the form of relatives do not usually come near. While they even avoid inviting one to functions, one should forget about the cordiality. Such experiences at home and in the society are responsible for dispiriting the minds of the elders.

The mind is gradually discouraged before the body suffers from lack of enthusiasm. High blood pressure, diabetes, joint pain, backache and waist pain and even grave ailments like cancer shamelessly make our body their home. Finally, even the brain and the nervous system may betray us.

Forgetfulness, shivering of the body, losing physical as well as mental balance for which one has to hold the walking stick and hear nasty comments from people are all the characteristic features of old age. Even if the eardrum is on strike one can particularly hear the critical comments made by others. Even if one is unable to watch good things or read good books because the vision has become considerably dim, one can see the look of disgust and contempt on the faces of people around.

The Oscillating Human Mind

The human mind constantly oscillates from one end of the spectrum of optimism to the other extreme, which is despondency. The human mind has the capacity to soar unimaginable heights. It keeps on changing every moment, happiness and positivity at one instant while it changes to sorrow or negativity in a moment. During the childhood phase of life the mind is happy most of the times while as age advances it starts feeling sadness more often. There are a number of reasons for the onset of depression in old age.

Ageing-

Changes related to the body, mind, family situations, sexual behavior and hormones take place during old age. The means of income as well as spending time are reduced due to retirement. This leads to loss of confidence. With the occurrence of diabetes, high blood pressure, cancer, Parkinsonism, dementia, Alzheimer which adorn the body like ornaments, the human mind feels dejected and gets pushed into the gorge of depression. Every living being has to go through this process of ageing. It is only the human being who is gifted with the ability to think about it and to worry about it. Many a times this otherwise valuable gift of the capability to think tortures the mind and the body.

Initially, ageing makes itself manifest either through a few silver strands in the hair or the receding hairline. Men develop a potbelly while women's waste lines expand, weight increases and their figure becomes unattractive. After this, the eyes and ears refuse to co-operate. The appetite is weak but since control on the tongue is missing, usually old people develop gas and fart. Owing to diabetes or enlarged prostate men feel the need to urinate often but do not feel completely relieved. Even the bowel movement in the morning is unsatisfactory.

Being able to recollect the name of the grandchild standing in front of you, only after going through the names of all grandchildren, or not being able to remember the name of the friend or relative one is actually talking to, is called Nominal Aphasia. There are frequent occasions when the glasses hang around the neck or are pushed up to the forehead and one is going around frantically hunting for them. This is the height of forgetfulness.

The body bends forward, knee and waist movement becomes very painful. The body and the mind tend to lose control very easily. All these changes lead to loss of self-confidence. The time required for learning new technology like use of smart phones, computers, electronic games or any new knowledge is too long and at times one feels an aversion towards learning. This is a gradual march towards total defeat on all fronts. However, the ego refuses to shrink. The feeling that,' I have taken all the decisions so far as head of the family, I am so experienced, so senior and so my headship should remain intact', continues to dominate the mind. If this feeling is not gratified, the tempers soar high leading to arguments or non-communication. If these measures do not help, the tension in the family escalates and the old are pushed into the valley of melancholy.

In the summer of youthfulness, the performance even on the sexual front is outstanding. Nevertheless, with advancing age the hormone levels dip low, the feeling of gratification is lowered, and finally it ends. The feeling that one has become useless on all fronts and in all capacities tortures the mind. In addition to this if high blood pressure, diabetes, cancer, or even aids have come to stay or one has booked one's passage to heaven by suffering from heart attack, paralysis then this feeling of depression is at its peak.

Similarly if one is required to separate from the joint family after one has already given everything in one's possession and death separates the couple, the ensuing loneliness is insurmountable. When emotional support is lost, a person is bound to drown in depression. The blood supply to the brain is reduced and the overall situation is very disheartening. In such circumstances, the only support, which can be found, is to take recourse in the grace of Almighty God. Such people are hooked on to spiritualism. They spend time in rituals, worship, chanting mantras, reading sacred books and participate in discussions on spiritual matters. Those who do not take this course sit idle, staring in the void and add to their depressive thoughts. They require other's help even in routine activities because of loss of appetite and sleep, increasing physical weakness and additional physical illnesses. They lose interest in life. Life seems a burden and the urge of self-protection, which is the prime necessity in the pyramid of evolution, is completely lost, leading to unnatural musings about suicide. If this depressive condition of the old person is not treated on time with the help of a psychiatrist, it can lead to the person actually committing suicide.

Remedy:

It is important to implement certain preventive measures so that depression does not set in or at least does not exceed its limits.

When children drive away their parents from their home, the husband and wife strongly support each other in those challenging circumstances. If the old people have someone by their side to express their emotions, to share their feelings they feel comfortable. If they go for daily walks, spend time in worship and prayer, confide their thoughts and feelings in each other they can render a strong support to each other. Nevertheless, Fate is supreme! We have no say against it. When one of the partner dies the other is faced with, the unbearable punishment of staying alone. Suddenly losing mental and physical support is like being robbed of the walking stick on which one's balance depended. But we must accept the inevitable. The show must go on.

We are all educated and mature people. We have been witness to the mental and physical changes that our earlier generations faced. Hence, we must keep in mind that we too will have to face these changes in the future.

Primary Needs

Life's primary needs are food, water and shelter. Only after these are fulfilled do the other needs become important.

Laila said to Majnu," I need you. I cannot survive without you."

Majnu replied."I am hungry, so I need food, I cannot live without food".

Laila was so disappointed.

Majnu explained," I have the necessary air, water and food. I wish to live a long life and will never desert you. I shall not be able to stay alive without you".

Laila was happy when she heard this. Both of them decided that they would use the available resources of air, water and food scrupulously, live a long life so that they would get enough time to love one another.

Air is the first requirement of life, after air, we need water and then food. Even if this is the truth about most of the living beings, there exist a few exceptions like anaerobic bacteria, which survive without air. Some organisms survive even in boiling hot lava. Scientists feel that, there could be some planets in the universe where this sequence is altered or is completely different. In short, this means that it is possible to survive without air, water, food and Laila. This is a scientific truth. However, let us understand the importance of basic needs for us in the sequence in which they are required.

Air – Man's most important need for survival is oxygen. Fortunately, we get this free of charge from the moment we are born until we breathe our last. We are ruining this gift of nature with our own hands. The statistics of air pollution and its increasing amount is proof that we are causing unlimited harm to our fellow beings, which can hardly be compensated. We are inviting numerous health related problems and endangering not only our lives but also the lives of future generations. Some awareness regarding these problems has been created but there are a lot many things, which can be avoided to curb air pollution.

Water – The second need for human survival in the order of importance is water. Our body contains about 75% of water. The brain and nervous system contains 85%, the blood has 80%and the muscles contain 70% of water. It is like water, water everywhere! In short, this means life is water.

Drinking water must be potable, clean and pure. The amount of impurities, microorganisms, chemicals, metals should be negligible. A normal person requires about 2.5 to 3 liters of water every day on an average. The oxygen mixed in the blood reaches all the cells because of water. Water makes it convenient to throw out of the body the waste products in the form of urine and excreta, resulting from the process of metabolism. Some of the waste products are excreted out of the lungs and skin. It is with the help of water that the skin, lungs and kidneys can maintain normal body temperature. Water means life, air also means life. It is difficult to describe their importance in words. The body receives water in limited measures from tea, coffee, milk, fruits and other food items but the major quantity is derived from drinking water. The body's need for water varies according to the change in geographical regions and climates.

Food – (For the old, eating should be considered as a religious act and not a pleasurable on.)

The third requirement for leading life is food. We all agree that food is divine and food is the complete deity. Food, water and air are divine! Man can satisfy his need for food with the help of various food items. A lot of research is continuously conducted regarding the right kind of food that can prove nutritious for the body. If we select accordingly, we can maintain health, longevity and satisfaction in life. Food is the fuel, which generates energy required to run the machine called the body.

If considered carefully we will realize that the single source of energy in Nature is sunlight and heat. Each small and large plant transforms sun energy into carbohydrates. The herbivorous animals get energy from the plants and the carnivorous animals devour these animals to get their share of energy. Man is omnivorous and consumes vegan food as grains, tubers and fruits and eggs, milk, fish and flesh that are produced from animals to satisfy his hunger. Even before the food cycle and its advantages for the body were understood, man ate various food items. Those who preferred non-vegetarian food consumed animal products such as milk, fats, flesh, fish and also jowar , bajra, sprouts, lentils, vegetables and fruits. Those who followed non-vegetarianism and believed in the principle of non-violence ate grains, vegetables, fruits and included only milk, which is an animal product in their diet. Prior to this, they included all the ingredients and had a square meal.

It did not matter much that people did not possess scientific knowledge about these foods. Nevertheless, it is a good thing that with scientific enquiry even the common person has now started considering the constituents of a nutritious meal, the ideal proportion of ingredients, and the frequency with which to consume them, after how many intervals and so on. It is now possible to select one's diet based on the amount of physical activity commensurate with age, exercise, economic conditions, climatic conditions, temperature and other factors. It is indeed advisable to consume a well balanced diet but it is also true that the workers who have just chaff for food are healthier and stronger than many.

Let us talk about the dietary needs of senior citizens. It is only proper that the people of advanced age must consume less food than when they were young. Instead of having just two sumptuous meals, they should divide their quota of food into four or five smaller meals. They should take their evening meals at least two and a half hours before going to bed. In our country, the Jains have their dinner before sun set. This practice is a very healthy one. In most of the developed countries, people have a heavy breakfast before leaving for work, have a very frugal lunch and eat dinner around seven in the evening after returning from work. Even this practice is a healthy one. We must gather information from doctors and nutritionists about the right proportion of proteins, carbohydrates, fatty foods and vitamins to be consumed in our diet and plan accordingly.

Proteins help us in developing immunity and in the growth and revitalizing of the body. While non-vegetarians get proteins from consuming fish, eggs, mutton, vegetarians get it from milk, curds, sprouts and lentils. Grains like wheat, rice, jowar, bajra and ragi are rich in carbohydrates and supply a small amount of proteins too. We receive our supply of proteins and carbohydrates through the twin combinations of curry and bhakri, chapatti, curry and rice or khichadi. Even if these combinations change due to geographical changes, yet we can ensure the supply of both proteins and carbohydrates. We receive the right quantity of fats through the oil that is used to season curries or sprouts and to prepare chapattis, butter taken with rice as also from milk, curds and butter. Green leafy vegetables, carrots, radish, beetroot, tomato, onion, garlic, cucumber all of them supply antioxidants when taken in a raw form or in the form of salads. They decelerate the ageing process and helps in postponing it. The body's requirement of vitamin C and minerals is satisfied through vegetables and fruits. Amla, oranges, sweet lime and tomato supply good amounts of vitamin C.

The World Health Organization has suggested that we require 60% carbohydrates, 20 % proteins and 20% fats in our daily diet. Dietitians are of the opinion that patients suffering from diabetes should reduce their intake of carbohydrates and those suffering from kidney ailments should cut down their intake of proteins.

Amino acid, Tyrosine is useful in brain functioning, thinking, alertness and the maintaining balance of the body. We can get it from non-vegetarian food, sprouts, soya bean, sesame and ground nuts. Obese people should use sesame, groundnuts moderately. Fats supply vitamins A, C, D and E. Those patients who suffer from high blood pressure and heart disease should choose fatty foods very carefully. It is possible to get High Density Cholesterol as well as Omega 3 fatty acids by consuming almonds, chestnut, rice bran oil, and olive oil and maintain the desired proportion of high density and low-density cholesterol in the blood. This scheme is useful for elderly patients with complaints such as blood pressure, heart disease and those whose arteries have contracted due to arthrosclerosis. If they eat two or three cloves of garlic every day, it can be of help. A recent study showed that the Jains who did not eat garlic and onions at all are more prone to these ailments.

Proteins are a source of amino acids. They are useful as raw material for preparing the neurotransmitters necessary for the functioning of the brain and the nervous system. The most important among them are tryptophan and tyrosine. They are found in fish, milk, eggs, cheese, wheat, oats, lentils and sprouts, unpolished red rice, fruits and vegetables. Tryptophan is essential for good sleep and hence consuming carbohydrates, milk and curds helps to produce it. The consumption of oil should be limited to half a liter per person in a month.

Milk, curds, oil, butter, fruits supply the necessary vitamins A, B, C, D, and E etc. Hence, one should include suitable amounts of vegetables, fruits and milk along with other food ingredients in their diet. Linseed, sprouted fenugreek seeds (even if they are bitter to taste), other sprouts, cowpeas and gram should also be included in the food consumed. Even oats, amaranth and sweet potatoes should be consumed depending on their availability.

People observe fasts for two reasons. One is a religious one and the other to rest the stomach. Following these religious principles such as good thoughts and behavior, unity, tolerance, renunciation, abstaining from stealing are beneficial to humankind. However, it cannot be credited to the benefits of observing a fast. It is believed that fasting might help in controlling the mind and the erotic impulses. If we consider the body, the stomach does not need any rest. Each cell in the body has to remain functional from the beginning to the end. If any one of these systems, the brain or the respiratory system or blood circulation or urinary system decide to take a holiday it will lead to dire consequences. Indians believe that consuming purgatives periodically is beneficial for health. Even this is a pointless, unsubstantiated claim. One should not overeat and if the bowel movement is not satisfactory, one must consult a doctor. Observing fasts and consuming laxatives both are unnecessary.

Recently scientists have found out that deficiency of vitamin B-12 and D-3 causes many ailments. It leads to symptoms such as considerable weakness, depression, pain in the muscles and joints. If this deficiency is found in the blood report, it is necessary to treat it with B-12 injections followed by a course of tablets that work like magic. The same is true of vitamin D- 3 deficiency. The calcium in the bones gets depleted in this condition.

There is a close relation between D-3 vitamin and cholesterol in the blood. In the presence of early morning sunlight, our skin makes use of cholesterol in the blood as raw material and produces vitamin D-3. Today we wake up late, travel in closed vehicles and avoid all contact with sunlight. This punishes our body. Reduction in D-3 leads to depletion of calcium in the bones, osteoporosis that is a very painful condition. The frequency of fractures increases and since cholesterol remains unused it gets deposited on the sides of our blood vessels and narrows them down resulting in high blood pressure, heart ailments, paralysis, kidney failure and multi organ failure also. This leads to prolonged illness and reduction in life span. Hence, the only punishment for avoiding sunlight is to expose oneself to sunlight. So wake up early in the morning. Sit out on the balcony in as less clothes as possible and spend lots of time having breakfast and reading newspapers. This will help to reduce cholesterol in the blood and vitamin D-3 will be prepared in the body. It is therefore a win-win situation!

Since calcium in the bones naturally reduces after menopause, osteoporosis is unavoidable in aged women. Along with painful bones, they suffer from brittle bones, which are broken very easily. Regular doses of calcium and D-3 tablets should be taken to avoid problems. Milk and bananas should be an intrinsic part of their diet.

In short, one can conclude that only after the basic needs of air, water and food are fulfilled man turns to love as a mental need.

Features of Exercise

The habit of exercising regularly has its own advantages. All of us whether children, youngsters or old require to exercise. All the organs in our body, cells and cell groups are engrossed in performing their allotted duties regularly. Dilly dallying is not allowed at all. The brain is the whole and sole manager of the entire body. It is under the direction of the brain that the body discharges all the functions. It is a very strict taskmaster. The principle, 'use it or lose it', is applicable to everyone. Constant movement is necessary to perform better.

Exercise –

Every cell performs its duty invisibly. One can easily see the work done by the muscles and joints. While we exercise we can overtly watch the muscles working but at the same time the processes of blood circulation and breathing are covertly accelerated. The brain is alerted. The body's extra demand for oxygen is satisfied through fast breathing. The blood system supplies the available additional oxygen and stored glucose to various organs according to their need. Usually the brain requires an extra amount of glucose and oxygen as well as the muscles in the body and of the heart. This is how exercise works to our advantage.

It is not possible to decide the manner and duration of exercise based on any one single criterion. It depends on the age of the person, the manner of work the person does, temperature and other climatic conditions, the amount of oxygen in the atmosphere (the oxygen level at altitudes) etc. Outdoor games played by children, going to the gym, swimming, sit-ups, surya namaskar, yoga exercises and spring exercises are some of the exercises, which suit our purpose. It is always necessary to plan exercise regimes for seniors very carefully. They usually suffer from pain in the neck, waist, back, joints, and diseases such as blood pressure, diseases of the lungs, diabetes and obesity. They must carefully consider this in consultation with the doctor before selecting the exercise regime.

It is advisable for the old to avoid outdoor games, running and intensive gym activities. Regular walks and if possible taking brisk walks, swimming, climbing up and down the staircase, yoga exercises, pranayam, surya namaskar in moderation are some of the exercises one can perform in varied combinations and duration according to the advice of the doctor. It is important that the amount of time spent in exercising should be abruptly but gradually increased. One should exercise only that much so as not to run out of breath, not to cause injury and not feel uneasy or experience chest pain. Swimming is a good option because in swimming there is less likelihood of experiencing injuries. Deep breathing done in a squatting position increases the efficiency of the lungs and supplies the body with a larger amount of oxygen. It also helps in concentration of the mind and making it anxiety free. The habit of performing yoga exercises if developed from childhood and continued in old age helps in reduces rigidity of muscles and enhances flexibility of the joints. Consequently, the severity of injuries caused by stretching or falling down is lessened. Even doing exercises done routinely in school proves to be of great help.

Physical exercises, yoga exercises and pranayam are very fruitful for ensuring the health of the brain. Exercises not only increase the supply of glucose and oxygen to the brain but also release serotonin and endorphin in the brain, which reduces stress. This helps in improving the immune system of the body, which in turn keeps diseases away. We can create an environment, which is conducive to creating good health and well-being within oneself as well as outside. Our interest in living life is enhanced and we are happy which also helps in increasing our life span. Such a person participates in social work and does work with interest. Such a person forgets his own sorrows and helps others in forgetting theirs. Those who can manage to dance and enjoy music should do so according to one's capacity. This will keep the mind contented and cheerful.

Along with physical exercises, it is also important that the old undertake mental exercises also which will tease the brain. Solving crosswords, puzzles, mobile electronic games, reading, writing, discussing, bhajans, attending speeches and lectures will be food for the brain. This helps to retain intellectual, thinking capacity and alacrity and keep disorders like Parkinsonism, dementia, Alzheimer at bay or at least postpones its occurrence. The old people can live with self-esteem and self-confidence.

Hence, friends, physical and mental exercises have a large number of advantages. There is nothing to lose by exercising regularly. It is a winning game. However, one must give up lethargy and decide to exercise regularly.

The devout should make it a point to visit temples situated far off from their house every day in the morning and attend bhajans or aarti during the evening. This helps in exercising as well as reinforcing one's spiritual feelings. Those who love to listen to music should hear music while exercising which will also reduce the monotony of the work out. It will reduce the boredom as well as keep the mind cheerful.

If the seniors do not know about yoga exercises or pranayam, they should perform them initially under the supervision of experts and then follow video tapes by Ramdevbaba or some such expert. But some people claim on television that after following the exercise routine and medicines suggested by the Baba they lost weight around twenty five kilograms in fifteen days or their blood pressure or sugar came down to normal in just eight to ten days. Do not believe such stories at all. I would urge everyone to believe only the doctor we consult and the investigation reports. Otherwise, it will lead to additional problems.

Mirth –

Mirth is the spring of happiness. It is evident in the innocent smile of a newborn child or in the coy beam of the beloved or in a grin as a response to a joke. All smiles are indicators of happiness. It is easily possible to hide feelings such as sexual attraction, anger, lust. However, it is difficult to conceal one's joy. Even if we try to mask our joy but the smile on the face, the glitter in the eyes reveals everything. Actually, we must try to hide that smirk which appears when someone is caught in a tight corner. Otherwise, one must laugh heartily, make others laugh and distribute the joy among all. It is not that a smile on the face makes it look happier but it induces happiness in the entire body. Scientific inquiry supports this view. Laughter reduces the level of stress hormones in the body. The increased pressure is lowered and comes to normal. The amount of the chemical endorphin increases in the brain and this improves our immune system thereby reducing the possibility of contacting an infectious disease and helps to control cancer. In short, laughter creates springs of enthusiasm in the entire body. The negativity in the mind is reduced and the urge to live increases.

It is necessary to increase the enthusiasm and the will to live, joyousness and immunity among old people. It is natural to feel sorry when after retirement the source of income gets reduced, intimate bonds are loosened and even the family relations get disturbed. However, the true human spirit lies in the fact that one is able to overcome this sorrow. Laughter clubs can help in solving this problem to some extent.

Fortunately, in India in the last few decades many laughter clubs have been established. A large number of senior citizens participate in them. If the seniors start their day with a stroll for exercise, chitchat with seniors like them, perform yoga exercises, pranayam and conclude it all with laughter they will spend their entire day enthusiastically. If the mind is pleased, the body supports it positively and helps in curbing sickness. Laughter is the best medicine!

Laughter reduces the stress hormones and improves immunity. The sensation of pain is lowered and muscles are relaxed. As it keeps control over high blood pressure heart disease, ailments of the brain are kept under control. Laughter plays an important role in developing communication with our relatives and colleagues. A feeling of being included in a group gives the person assurance of being accepted as member. Differences with others are also reduced.

Laughter is more infectious than an epidemic. If we share happiness, it grows, while if we share sorrow it gets divided. One should distribute joy and get joy in return. It will not cause any loss to anyone. Become a member of the laughter club, which distributes joy to everyone. Watch comic shows, read comic books and laugh to your hearts' content. Laugh but do not grow fat!

Dr. Madan Katariya, an Indian doctor first started the concept of a laughter club in 1990 with a handful of friends in a garden in Mumbai. In 1995, 'Hasya Yog Club', became a proper movement. It then spread all over the world. In a survey taken in 2011 there are more than 8000 laughter clubs which function in hundred countries of the world. Every club has its own leader. A majority of the members of these clubs are senior citizens. They begin with warming up exercises, pranayam, yoga exercises which prepares their body and mind. They form a circle and start running round recalling their childhood days. The general etiquettes followed while laughing loudly in public are ignored. This helps to forget worries, stress and tensions and the laughter, which is, initially a guffaw begins to bloom gradually in a rising crescendo until people start rolling in laughter. The exercise concludes with a thunderous laugh. The various types of laughter require about twenty minutes. This helps the body feel light and cheerful. If this is followed by meditation or shawasan (an exercise in yoga), it creates a new exhilaration in the body as well as the mind.

Research conducted on this topic explains that physical exercises, pranayam, yoga and laughter supply extra oxygen to the brain. It also accelerates blood circulation and increases the quantity. We experience an emotion of ecstasy when the brain receives ample oxygen along with increased production of endorphin. The amount of stress hormones is also lessened. Consequently, we can control the feelings of worry, stress, frustration which otherwise torture the mind. Even the sensation of pain is reduced. According to an Oxford University scientist, endorphin works like opium, a painkiller. This study compared the effects of laughter club on its members with other controlled groups and came to this conclusion.

Many scientists feel that if laughter clubs are established all over the world it will help to increase fellow feeling, unconditional love, forgiveness and generosity among fellow beings and help to establish world peace.

It used to be said in the past that, a person who laughed without reason must be a crazy fellow. Now we must change that and appeal to all,' come together, derive happiness and laugh without reason'.

One thing is true that a hearty laugh is an exercise and a good practice.

Money Matters of Senior Citizens

The number of senior citizens has considerably increased on the global level due to improved life expectancy. The constant progress in health care will also help to raise it further. This is going to lead to serious economic issues for both the developed as well as under developed countries.

A hundred years ago, the joint family system was in vogue. The number of elders was comparatively less and they would be very dependent on the younger generation after their retirement. They were hardly worried about earning for a living or being looked after during sickness. Nevertheless, gradually as we progressed materially and materialism took firm root initially the developed countries and later even the under developed countries gave up the joint family system. This affected both the old and the new generations in small or large measure. The elders have had to give up on familial joy, love and security. The economic picture is still more alarming. The financial issues they face and the problems which arise have increased manifold and seem to increase by the day.

A popular saying goes, 'child is the father of man.' This may be true or not, but the present youth have already sensed their problems, which they would face when they grow old. This has a positive aspect also. The old people in the past would be at ease about their future. They would be careless in their young days about financial planning for the twilight of their life. The employed would be under the impression that they would be able to subsist on their pension and gratuity amount and would happily hand over their savings, their land, home everything in their possession to the younger generation. Gradually there was a change in these views. I am always reminded of a sentence from the play 'Natsamrat' that has created a great impact on my mind. 'One may give away the dish one is eating from, but one must never give up the chair one is sitting in!' When it first came, this play proved a revelation for many senior citizens. Not everyone agreed to it. Nevertheless, the younger generation woke up to face the reality. The advantage of this is that right from young age they are now becoming aware of the need to plan various means of ensuring a happy retired life.

If members of the earlier generation were well off, they invested in gold and land. They also started making investments in banks in the form of fixed deposits. The present generation is very thoughtful when it comes to financial planning. 'Retirement planning' has become the key word today. The importance of gold or fixed deposits has come down considerably. If we compare the returns on gold or deposits with the inflation rate the returns on investments is negligible. Due to the reduction in the purity of gold ornaments, loss of making charges, the danger of theft and fear of loss this investment is not lucrative. In the past forty or fifty years a new option in the form of company shares or mutual funds has become available all over the world. Life Insurance is another alternative. In the eventuality of sudden death if the person has borrowed a loan for the house or business, insurance claims help a lot. However, insurance as mere investment does not fetch enough profit.

If we study the long-term history of stock markets all over the world, we can see that investment in long-term shares made after consulting financial experts gives best returns. The younger generation has many investment options now. Alternative plans are available so that hard cash is at hand when needed, such as for children's education and higher education, wedding and other ceremonies in the family and so on. The principle suggested in the saying, 'Do not keep all the eggs in one basket', is applicable in case of investments also. Investment experts suggest that it is advisable to follow this adage and invest separately in gold, bank deposits, residential property, office or business location, insurance, mutual funds and shares. It is possible to follow this precaution when one's basket is full. However, those economically weak people who find it difficult to make both ends meet cannot even think of investing money. About sixty-five percent of the Indian population is financially incapable of any such thought. So now, with this background in mind let us consider the financial planning for the old.

The old belong to diverse economic groups. The 2014 census notes that sixty eight percent of the Indian population lives in villages. Most of them are framers or workers. Even if the percentage of school going children is ninety-six percent in the villages, yet the population above the age of sixty-five is largely illiterate. Their income is barely enough for them to manage food and shelter. They cannot think about the future arrangements, or plan financial preparedness for old age in the meager income they receive. Hence they are left with no other option but to depend upon their children in old age. They are compelled to stay in the village with their children or join them in the city if they have migrated or survive on the small amount of money sent by their children.

Senior Citizen Group –

According to the English saying , 'birds of a feather flock together', people who share the same characteristics and habits, ,or belong to the same caste or religion stay together. Those birds, beasts or humans who share the same joys and sorrows form groups and exist together. The problems and pleasures of retired people are similar and they have enough free time to come together. This is the principle behind formation of senior citizen groups.

Initially the people who retired from government and semi -government institutions came together for solving their problems related to pension. Gradually it spread to different places and slowly even those seniors who were not salaried but had set up businesses and now had retired due to age from them as well as family responsibilities, also joined these groups. As this movement grew, various regional, central and departmental employees formed their own groups. The major objective of each of them was to gather, share each other's joys and sorrows, and comfort one another. Usually all men retire from office work. A working woman might seek super annuity from her office work but she can never retire from her role as a home maker, wife and mother. The Marathi play, 'Aai Retire Hote' throws important light on this subject. Nevertheless, in a country full of villages like India those men and women who stay in the rural areas do not have recourse to retirement schemes or any associations related to that. Recently the government of India has declared a policy, which looks after the well-being of senior citizens. It is unfortunate that the benefits of such policies do not reach those who really need and deserve them.

Pension Scheme –

'Pension' is the payment that the employees who retire

from the government and semi-government institutions receive after their retirement. In order to receive the benefits of the pension scheme it is necessary to have completed at least ten years of continuous government service. The employees receive thirty percent of the last pay drawn as pension. After the death of the employee the spouse or whoever is the legally accepted nominee receives the pension. The amount of pension is deposited in the pension holder's post or bank account by the end of every month. The important condition is that periodically the pensioner is required to submit a life certificate proving that she or he is alive. Just as dearness allowance is paid to employees who are in service it is also paid to pensioners. This scheme gives the aged pension holder a good financial support.

Strange are the ways of the changing times! Once a person becomes permanent in the government job, the person starts making money through taking bribes. This income is very important according to them. The amount of bribe exceeds the salary so as to make the salary look unimportant. This generates a lot of black money and corrupt people are likely to spoil their children. The politicians who have reached heights of fraudulence seldom make any efforts to curb corruption. They have neither the moral right nor the political will to do so. Most of the times, they are hand in gloves with the government officers and collect bribe through them. Hence, it is convenient for both to keep mum on the topic. In fact, such unethical behavior is becoming the norm of the day. This leads to generating black money, depositing it in foreign banks and then bringing it back into the country through illegal means. This black money then gets invested in land and other things.

The Government of India declared 'Shrawan Baal Seva Rajya Nivrutti Yojna' for the benefit of old people above the age of sixty five. According to the details of this policy, the government arranges to give salary or maintenance for these old people without any support. Nevertheless, getting proper information about the policy, making a proper follow up and actually getting the benefits after subverting the corrupt system is an arduous task.

Besides financial support, these retired employees and poor politicians are generously given medical facilities. The politicians help the retired employees liberally with a view to receiving similar facilities in the future. In recent times government has adopted a broader outlook. It has started 'Shrawanbaal Seva Rjya Nivrutti Yojna', 'Indira Gandhi Vrudhapkal Nivrutti Yojna', 'Rajiv Gandhi Jeevandayi Arogya Yojna', financial aid from the government for patients suffering from heart related problems, cancer and kidney failure. If the seniors are aware of these schemes and are ready to struggle for them and persevere, a few of them may avail of these benefits. They should also have the ability to bribe the authorities otherwise; all their efforts will be wasted.

The population of India is about 125 million people. About ten percent of this population falls under the category of senior citizens. Only a maximum of twenty percent of these senior citizens get the benefit of pension schemes. This leaves eighty percent of seniors without any salary or pension. Today this figure which is around nine to ten million is going to increase further. Among them, there are very few very people who are rich. A large number belongs to the lower middle class or even the financially weaker section of society. The condition of senior citizens, in cities or villages, who belong to this financially weak category, is very pathetic. The more fortunate are able to get support from their families but the less fortunate have to resign to their fate and undergo suffering or then if it becomes too unbearable commit suicide.

Those who are not government employees and members of lower income groups face numerous problems because they are not entitled to any pension. Those who belong to higher income groups and have invested their savings in schemes, which give good returns, need not worry about financial matters. Since they have money with them, they attract their heirs, relatives, friends and other people who are willing to help them. They can also afford to appoint servants who look after their needs and comforts. In recent times, there have been instances in which relatives or servants have robbed or even murdered the senior citizens for their money and then absconded.

It is necessary that we prepare our will on time. It is wrong to presume that the will should be prepared when the end of life arrives. No one can predict when this last moment will turn up. When a fatal accident takes place, or one suffers a heart stroke, there is no scope for saving the person. Hence every person, especially a person with a family should prepare her or his will at an early stage in life. You have the right to make suitable changes whenever you wish to. If you make a will at a later stage it should be registered. Many a times relatives take objection to the details in the will after the death of the person, leading to many quarrels and litigations. In order to avoid such scandalous situations, nowadays, the option of preparing a trust while one is alive and managing one's property through that trust is available. You can consider this alternative with the guidance of an able finance consultant. If the will is not prepared and the person is on deathbed, then relatives have very little time to think. They make haste and take advantage of the situation by procuring signatures or thumb impressions of the dying person. Hence, to avoid any such mishaps it is advisable to be prepared beforehand.

Unburdening oneself emotionally, sharing joys and sorrows with others, passing time all are types of entertainment. For those seniors who are financially well placed, physically and mentally, fit, it is possible to earn money by doing part time jobs or undertaking some work for rendering free social service. They will feel happy, as they will be able to fulfill their social responsibility. In the cities, pensioner forums take interest in solving the problems of the elders. They arrange lectures by experts from among them, or music programmes or some such useful activity. They can undertake social service also. Some charitable trusts have already undertaken some such ventures (Sarvodaya Senior Citizen's General Forum).

NRIPO-

A large number of youngsters who are unskilled, illiterate, highly educated, intelligent or skilled have gone abroad either to the Middle East countries or any of the developed and developing countries, temporarily or permanently settled there in search of a living. They are prepared to live a thrifty life, work hard and hence they earn well. It is a matter of relief and satisfaction that these youth send money to their parents or family regularly. The Government of India gets a lot of foreign currency because of this. The Indian seniors get a lot of support through such money transfer. It also encourages foreign investment in India.

Parents of such non-residential Indians have come together and formed an NRI Organization called NRIPO. Some of the advantages of NRIPO are that the seniors meet each other, try to understand and if possible solve their problems, discuss about important issues, exchange joys and sorrows. NRIPO has a number of branches all over India.

Planning One's Retirement-

Everyone should keep in mind that after retirement the income is reduced or is even stopped. Therefore, it is very necessary to plan one's finances by investing in insurance, fixed deposits, company shares, mutual funds and similar sources whose returns will ensure sufficient income necessary after retirement. Those members, who earn well look after the educational, marriage and other needs of the family, build their own house either with or without borrowing loans. Even if the home loan is pending when one retires, it should be insured and all other loans should be repaid before retiring. If the finances are carefully planned, health insurance premium regularly paid then it means that one has prepared for post retirement expenses. We should not depend upon the next generation for these requirements.

If the arrangements one has made fall short of the requirements due to inflation, one has the option of reverse mortgaging one's own house property.

Home Loan-

When one does not have enough money to buy a house one spends money on a rented house. Instead of paying rent if we borrow a long-term loan we may have to pay a larger amount of money, larger than the rent but at the end we can get a double advantage i.e., the satisfaction of saving money and owning the house. Owing to the noble view of the government that everyone should own a house, banks, home loan societies and other agencies are willing to give long-term loans on reduced interest rates. Until the loan is repaid with interest, the house remains mortgaged with the bank. Considering the possibility of sudden, untimely death of the customer, the bank insists on ensuring that the loan amount is insured. Even this is beneficial because in case of any such eventuality the surviving family does not have to face the possibility of losing shelter.

Reverse Mortgage-

The government of India began this plan in 2007 in order to help the senior citizens. In the usual home loan plans, we get a loan first and then the house while in reverse mortgage scheme one has the house first on which loan is given. The valuer or valuer firm, which is appointed by the government, inspect and decide the value of the property. The bank offers sixty percent of this amount determined by the valuer either in total or in installments to the owner. The borrower and her or his partner can live in that house for their whole life. The house is valued from time to time. This facility of reverse mortgage is available only for those seniors who are above sixty years of age.

Those who get the total amount at one go can utilize that amount either for other savings, or for personal expenses. But they have to repay the loan installment along with the interest every month. Instead, if the amount is borrowed on monthly installment basis the amount can be useful like pension or salary amount. The tenure of this scheme usually is fifteen years but it could be even twenty years in certain exceptional cases.

Those senior citizens, who do not enjoy the benefits of pension schemes, do not have enough savings, whose children do not help or support them, or those who do not have any children at all, are eligible to avail of this scheme. The possibility is that the house may survive after them but they would not have enough means to support themselves when they are alive. In such cases rather than suffering from unsatisfied needs they can avail of this reverse mortgage scheme and spend their life free of hassles. In case of the death of one of the partners, the other can continue to enjoy the house as well as installments. After the death of both, the successor mentioned in the will can get the house after repaying the entire loan amount with interest. Whether they have children or not, those seniors who avail of the reverse mortgage plan, mention in their will the person or institution that is to receive the amount left after the bank disposes the house and deducts the loan amount from that money. Banks follow the instructions given in the will. If the person has not made a will, then the bank distributes the amount among those beneficiaries whose names are mentioned in the bank agreement documents, while taking the loan. If the borrower wishes to change the names of beneficiaries she or he can change them. One can change the will anytime before one's death.

In short, we can say that if in spite of physical, mental weakness due to ageing, if one adopts a positive point of view then the period of old age can be lived happily.

The four-letter word 'plan', is very important in everyone's life. This planning can be made regarding health or minor events or major issues such as financial ones. One is required to plan in every aspect of life. Planning therefore does not have an alternative but to plan.

Maladies of Old Age

10

Every disease is impartial. It does not make any difference between sex, age, religion, caste, region or country. Yet there are some diseases, which are gender specific. Even if some of them are age related problems, they may occur at any age. Many of the ailments can be different in different ages and genders. Some of them can even be typical of certain geographical regions; climates and occurrence of insects in those areas. They also depend upon the level of cleanliness, use of vaccines and the epidemics, which break out in those areas.

Every one wishes to remain away from diseases but that is not always possible. We consider our own problems as too large to counter while the other's problems are insignificant.

We are going to consider the health related problems of elders in this book.

Eyes: The eye is an important organ. If we blindfold ourselves and try to move around for a day or two we will be able to experience the awful challenges faced by the blind. Queen Gandhari who in spite of having normal eyesight decided to blindfold her eyes to experience the tribulations of her blind husband, must be considered as a great person. The efficiency of the brain, thought processes and other sense organs is amplified in those who are blind by birth and that helps them to live quite a normal life. They are able to surmount their physical limitations.

With advancing age, when one approaches one's forties, the capacity of the eyes to accommodate the focus reduces and it becomes necessary to wear spectacles for reading or seeing objects, which are close. Later in the sixties problems such as cataract, glaucoma occur and can cause blindness. However, they can be treated and cured completely .This will help to avoid the impending blindness.

Cataract: The increasing opacity of the lens in the eyes causes cataract. Clean, clear lenses get clouded and become unclear. This results in gradually diminishing eyesight and finally leads to blindness. Diabetic patients and those who have suffered eye injuries can suffer from cataract at an early age. Even those people who are on steroids for a long time, are also likely to suffer from cataract and glaucoma. It is possible to replace the opaque lens with a fabricated one that is able to restore the vision completely. This surgery has now become quite easy and effective.

Glaucoma-

The occurrence of Glaucoma is quite frequent in old people. When the flow of the transparent fluid in the eye, Aqueous humor, is obstructed the pressure in the eye increases which causes Glaucoma. If treated properly by an expert, the impending blindness caused due to Glaucoma can be avoided through proper medication and surgery if required.

If high blood pressure and diabetes are not properly controlled, it causes the small blood vessels in the eye to rupture and even this can cause blindness. In order to avoid this it is important to keep good control on diabetes and blood pressure. This condition is treated with the help of laser surgery with partial success.

Ears-

It is a precious gift to be able to hear properly. Hearing helps us to communicate with others as well as avoid accidents. We can listen to music. As we move towards old age, there occur degenerative changes in the ear, which reduces the capacity to hear. A few people become completely deaf but in most old people, partial deafness sets in. Such loss of hearing leads to misunderstanding among the people around and especially between husband and wife and creates a lot of confusion.

"You do not pay enough attention to what I speak." "You have lost interest in me," are some of the examples of misapprehensions developed due to hearing deficiency. It is necessary to consult the doctor who can suggest the use of hearing aids that will avoid misinterpretation.

High Blood Pressure/Heart Disease –

With advancing age when the flexibility of the arteries is reduced and Arteriosclerosis, i.e., rigidity of the arteries causes increase in blood pressure. This process of hardening begins in childhood, continues slowly in youth and gets accelerated in old age. A majority of senior citizens suffer from high blood pressure. Excessive consumption of salt, sweet meats, oil, butter and other fatty foods in young age leads to an early occurrence of high blood pressure. Obesity and heredity also play an important role in triggering off high blood pressure. People who consume tobacco in any form and those who lead a life of stress and tension are more prone to suffer from high blood pressure at an early stage.

Diabetes-

The percentage of glucose in the blood is found to be higher in those people who have a history of diabetes, who are obese and who are temperamentally lethargic. Diabetes prefers sluggish, inactive people.

The arteries in the body get narrower in the case of both high blood pressure and diabetes. All the important organs like the heart, brain, kidneys get affected and it leads to fatal diseases such as heart attack, paralysis and kidney failure.

Those who do not exercise regularly suffer from calcium deficiency that leads to brittle bones. They are likely to suffer from muscle pain, joint pain, and fractures very easily. Even a small fall leads to major fractures. In such cases, surgeries have to be conducted even if the senior citizen's general health condition is not very good. In obese people, before their weight affects the ground it has already ruined the knee joint. When knee pain becomes unbearable and instead of the youthful swan like gait when one starts to sway like a boat, replacement of the knee joint becomes inevitable. In order to avoid this it is necessary to exercise regularly and reduce the intake of oil, ghee, butter and sweets. If the bones have less calcium or D-3 and B-12 it can be supplemented by taking calcium, D-3, B-12 tablets according to the physician's recommendations.

Ailments of the Brain-

Diseases like increase in absentmindedness, Parkinsonism, Alzheimer's occur due to degenerative changes in the brain. We cannot avoid them completely but regular physical and mental exercise, a healthy diet, sound sleep, treatment for high blood pressure and diabetes on time and being cheerful by keeping stress and tension away, can help to minimize them or delay their onset.

It is quite easy to prescribe such doses of wisdom but bringing the suggestions into practice is a difficult job. Even if this is true one must sincerely try to follow these prudent words.

Cancer-

Everyone is disturbed and scared by the mere mention of the name Cancer. The possibility of occurrence of cancer increases with advancing age. The only exception to this is 'blastoma' which develops in childhood and 'sarcoma' which arises at a very young age, both are types of cancers. Almost all other types of cancers happen in old age. Cancers could sometimes be gender specific also. In women breast cancer, cancer of the uterus and the ovary are quite common while men suffer from prostate and testicle cancer. Breast cancer occurs very rarely in men. Incidence of other cancers such as mouth cancer, cancer of the food pipe, stomach, large intestine, kidney, liver, thyroid or any other organ is seen in both men as well as women. Consuming tobacco, smoking or anything, which causes reduced immunity, is reason enough for causing cancer.

If with the help of regular exercises, a balanced diet, yoga exercises, pranayam and meditation we succeed in reducing stress and tension, keep our mind cheerful by listening to music and watching dance and remain away from addictions we will be able to improve our power of resistance. Every one, big and small should be aware of the fact that improved power of resistance certainly helps in avoiding cancer or at least helps to fight against it successfully.

Considering that in the initial stages cancer is not painful everyone should note that any unwanted new growth or injury which does not cause pain should be immediately referred to an expert doctor. In fact, we should consult a good doctor in the incidence of any malady and should carefully follow the advice given by the doctor immediately. It is all right to get more information about the disease with the help of the internet but half knowledge can be a dangerous thing. Do not make the mistake of considering oneself as a doctor based on information gathered from the internet.

Sleep-

Human body primarily requires air, water and rest. The importance of sleep is evident in the fact that the need for food comes after sleep. Few people know that man can stay alive without food for fifteen days but not for long without sleep.

Enlargement of the Prostate-Prostate glands are situated at the entrance of the urinary tract in all men. These glands are likely to enlarge around the age of sixty. It causes increase in the number of times one is required to urinate in the night time. It also causes problems such as delay in urine flow or unsatisfactory urine discharge. This leads to frequent visits to the urinal, obstructed urine flow or lack of control over urine discharge because of which the person cannot control himself and urinates even before reaching the toilet. The person suffers frequently from urine infection, which leads to repeated urination and cold and fever.

Prostate enlargement may be due to cancer as well as some other reasons. On the advice of an expert urologist, one must get one's urine checked, undergo sonography tests and PSA test which is necessary to diagnose prostate cancer and follow the treatment suggested. Prostate cancer can be treated with surgery but chemotherapy also proves effective.

Breast Cancer-

Occurrence of breast cancer is widely spread among women all over the world. Studies reveal that women who have not breast fed their children are comparatively more susceptible to breast cancer. If a cancerous lump develops in the breast, there are no indications of pain or any other symptoms for a long time. Hence, one tends to ignore it. In a country like India, women are shy and defer visiting a doctor. They should strictly avoid this tendency to postpone consulting a physician. Even if they do not suffer from any discomfort, all women must learn from their familiar surgeon how to examine one's breasts for the possibility of cancer. They must stand before the bathroom mirror and conduct self-examination at least twice a month. If we can detect breast cancer in its early stages, we can treat it with surgery and chemotherapy .It can be cured completely. This will avert any untoward happening. Both the treatments ensure the promise of a long life ahead.

Alzheimer-

The capacity to remember declines as one grows old. Many patients start forgetting things almost in their fifties. This is termed as dementia. Age destroys the neurons in the brain and new ones are not produced to replace them. Those individuals in whose case this process is accelerated in the fifties itself are said to be suffering from 'dementia' or 'Alzheimer's' disease. The occurrence of this disease is three to four times greater in women than in men. A person suffering from Alzheimer's has hardly six to twelve years of life left after its onset. An early diagnosis of this disease helps to increase the life of the patient. Regular physical exercises (for one to two hours daily) along with mental exercises such as solving quizzes, reading, playing games which involve intelligence, a balanced healthy diet, living in a happy environment and avoiding stress and tension and totally abstaining from addiction of any kind ensures an extension to the patient's duration of life up to a certain limit. Does suffering from Alzheimer's mean that the patient has gone mad? If we cannot cure the disease why treat it at all? Such questions are completely incorrect. Every individual has the right to live as long as possible. Therefore, the person's relatives and doctors should make all the necessary efforts for ensuring this. It may be difficult to diagnose this disease but it is not impossible. The patient's history, details about her or his behavior as described by close relatives, absence of other diseases, investigations such as C.T., MRI scans all help in the diagnosis.

Even if death is inevitable yet proper treatment for blood pressure and diabetes, controlling cholesterol levels, reducing the intake of salt, sugar and fatty foods is necessary. It is advisable to avoid weight gain. Consume B-12 and D-3 tablets according to the doctor's advice.

Angioplasty-Bypass Surgery-

The importance of heart disease is unparalleled in the lives of the aged. Even the common person is well acquainted with the terms angioplasty and bypass surgery. Along with ageing, the arteries are constricted. When the coronary artery that supplies blood to the muscles of the heart is contracted and clogged, that causes chest pain. When this constriction increases the blood supply to the heart muscles is considerably reduced, or is even stopped and that causes the death of the heart muscles. This eventuality is termed as 'heart attack'. Heart attack can prove fatal in the case of many patients. In order to avoid this we must concentrate on controlling diabetes, high blood pressure, maintaining cholesterol levels, keeping stress and tension at bay, refraining from any type of tobacco consumption, controlling weight gain and following a regular exercise pattern. In spite of this if there develop blockages in the coronary artery leading to chest pain or breathlessness one must consult a doctor immediately. In order to widen the path of the constriction it is first inflated and a stent is inserted which helps in increasing the flow of blood. But if there are multiple blockages in the two main coronary arteries or their subordinate blood vessels, then it becomes necessary to graft arteries or veins from other parts of the body and create an alternative path. This is termed as 'bypass' surgery. This is done as open-heart surgery or laparoscopic surgery. Due to recent developments in diagnostic tests, anesthesia and surgical procedures minimum risk is incurred in this operation.

After treatment, the patient gets a heart that is younger by ten to fifteen years and is once again ready for non-stop work. The surgery can be repeated if need arises. In recent times, because life expectancy has increased these cures have become a necessity.

Joint Replacement-

The increase in human longevity is a mixed fruit basket. It may have its advantages but there are also a number of disadvantages. The process of ageing reduces calcium in the bones, especially in women. Reduced calcium leads to fragile bones. Such bones can very easily develop fractures if the person just falls down or is slightly hurt. When they reach the age, of seventy, eighty or ninety all their bodily functions have already become very weak and many diseases have found a home in their body. If they are bedridden for a long period a painful death from pneumonia and bedsores is inevitable. Hence, even if we incur a lot of risk, we can conduct joint replacement surgeries on such patients. If these surgeries are successful, the old are able to carry on independently with their activities for a few more years. They can lead a pain free life.

Very old people are required to replace their hip joints. Knee replacement surgery is done on younger senior citizens. They suffer excruciating pain in the knee joint because of wear and tear. Nowadays knee replacement is made on both the knees simultaneously. As the patients are sixty to seventy years, old after surgery they can walk through a pain free life liberated from knee pain. They have to face some inconvenience, as not being able to squat on the floor. Since the elders live for a longer time they may have to undergo joint replacement surgeries a second time in life.

Constipation-

As age advances, our organs slacken down. Muscles become weak. The muscles of the intestine also are not an exception to this rule. Even they become feeble and their movement becomes sluggish. Consequently, the food is not properly digested. The waste products in the intestine are pushed out very slowly and are not thrown out easily. This is termed as 'constipation'. Constipation is not a disease but a symptom of failure to excrete properly which occurs due to ageing. This causes flatulency also. Sometimes owing to the inability to pass stools, the excreta gets collected and causes fecal impaction. A weak large intestine and rectum are unable to excrete it. The subsequent excreta, which is in a liquid form gets disposed off from the sides of the accumulated the impaction giving the patient a feeling of loose motions and loss of control over the bowel movement.

In such cases the excreta has to be removed physically under anesthesia or without, by inserting gloved fingers or even without gloves into the rectum and breaking it into small pieces. Later enema is given twice daily to ensure that the large intestine has been emptied of all waste matter. This entire process is extremely painful but has to be done in acute cases of constipation. Patients are then asked to include fiber rich green leafy vegetables, carrots, radish and fruits in their diet.

Some senior patients of constipation regularly remove the excreta using their own hands. After some time this becomes not only a habit but an addiction. This might lead to injuries to the rectum and large amount of blood loss. Patients must take proper care that they do not indulge in any such habit and seek proper medical guidance.

Frozen shoulder –

After one crosses fifty years of age, movements of one of the shoulders or both of them like raising the hands above the head or tying them behind become very painful and the range gets restricted. There are no overt symptoms like swelling on the shoulders or any other visible changes. These changes are not even evident in X-ray examination but the pain is unbearable.

Some times in some cases, this pain subsides by itself. Physiotherapy exercises reduce the pain in two weeks and gradually we can achieve complete relief from pain.

Waist and Neck Pain-

The changes caused by ageing affect the spinal cord also and the cartilage, which acts as a cushion in between two spines, wears away. The nerves that run through the spinal cord are compressed and the area related to these experience pain. Usually more pain occurs in the neck and waist region. Soreness, a tingling sensation, numbness and weakness of the muscles are some of the problems faced by the aged in this ascending sequence. If we learn exercises required for the neck and back and follow them carefully, we can experience a lot of relief. If the cartilage is worn out considerably, it is necessary to consult an expert and go in for surgery according to the doctor's advice. Some of these operations are now possible with the help of laparoscopic surgery that helps in reducing pain and expenses and hospitalization.

Cramps-

The calf muscles suddenly contract during the daytime or in the night and cause agonizing pain. This is called as spasm or cramp. The exact reason for such contraction is not known but reduced levels of calcium and E vitamin deficiency could be some of the causes. Doses of Vitamin E and Calcium tablets could help in curing cramps. It is possible that cramps occur in not only the calf muscles but other muscles of the body too.

Vitamins and Minerals-Building Homes in the Sun-

In order that our body receives the necessary nutrition of proteins, carbohydrates, fats and the right proportion of vitamins, minerals we must plan our diet accordingly. Even if we miss any of these ingredients, we are likely to suffer from various diseases.

If the seniors' intake of iron is deficient, they suffer from anemia. Researchers have recently found out that deficiency of B-12 and D-3 leads to different maladies such as primarily general weakness, feeble muscles, joint and waist pain and lack of enthusiasm. If deficiency of vitamins and minerals is found in the blood after relevant tests are conducted, the deficiency can be treated by administering vitamins and minerals in the diet and medicine. This gives enormous relief from all the earlier mentioned symptoms. If you sit out in the open, exposed to the early morning sunlight, your skin converts the cholesterol in the blood to vitamin D-3.This has a twofold advantage as it increases the amount of D-3 in the blood and reduces cholesterol. We must consider that these problems are inevitable in old age and must seek the doctor's advice as soon as these symptoms become evident.

It is advisable to adopt a life style, which enables us to take care and prevent illnesses before they occur rather than treat them after they have surfaced.

Ageing

11

The constant growth of the human body, which takes place on a daily basis, is termed as 'ageing'. It is an intrinsic part of everyone's life. By the end of the childhood period, the physical capacity of the human body naturally starts diminishing but the capacity to learn, the competence to use one's experience to surmount all odds is increased. These capabilities do not vanish immediately with retirement. Many people remain physically and mentally fit even after the age of sixty and they can serve society as well as guide the young. Even the nation's economy and social planning can be benefitted by their contribution. History is rife with examples of great men above the age of seventy and eighty or even after that who have enriched society by dedicating their music, artifacts, literature or scientific discoveries. Such examples are comparatively less in number.

Usually after the age of sixty, the physical and mental ability starts to weaken and it is quite possible that these elders become victims of various diseases. These senior members have every right to lead a respectable life. We must acknowledge the importance of their service, which they rendered to the nation and society in their youthful days, and so it is the duty of every nation and society to look after their wellbeing in their old age. Care should be taken that they are not ignored. It is the responsibility of the government to implement strict measures to ensure that they are not exploited, cheated or oppressed.

The Art of Ageing-

Everyone will agree that dance, music, painting or for that matter any art enriches human life. Art also helps in extending artists' life till old age. The only condition is that the artist should not be addicted to tobacco or other narcotic drugs. You may wonder about what is the relationship between art and ageing. Every art gives us pleasure. The brain of the person who indulges in arts produces the chemical endorphin in a larger quantity. It creates the feeling of joy in the person's mind and the person is lost in happiness. This has a very positive effect on the entire body. The immune system of the body is activated and the level of stress hormones in the blood is reduced. This helps in maintaining normal levels of high blood pressure and sugar. When these two enemies are under control and good immunity is able to win the battle against infections and cancer we are able to curb a number of ailments. The person can enjoy a long life and age gracefully. If the person is not an artist yet with the help of workout, yoga, laughter clubs, meditation and all such means can keep the stress hormones at a lower level and live a long life. This can be made possible by following a happy life style, increasing the endorphin level and remaining cheerful always. Friends, the mantra for ageing, longevity is, 'Be merry and make merry'.

In youth when one is living a healthy life, no one thinks about death. But a silver streak in the hair, balding and hair loss, wrinkles on the skin, dental problems, joint pains, receding sexual urge, a bent back which are all signs of advancing age disturb the mind. They proclaim the onslaught of old age. The shadow of death pervades the mind and then the person wakes up to the alarm. She or he tries to hide one's age by using artificial measures such as colouring one's hair or applying creams to the skin. Nevertheless, these measures do not lessen the fear of death, which constantly haunts the person's mind. This makes her or him perennially sad. Rather than feeling sad, it is better to age happily by reducing the pace of ageing though one cannot avoid death completely. Arts, spirituality, keeping fit, engaging in some hobby, going on pilgrimages or visiting beautiful natural spots or any such activity which will keep your mind cheerful, all help in increasing a happy life span. If we implement these measures knowingly or unknowingly we can ensure that contented ageing is achieved. Positive thoughts, emotions, and arts have a very important role to play in our life. Those of us who have ignored this will find that signs of ageing become manifest in them very early. Even if they accept a positive attitude and keep away from addiction, they can yet achieve happy ageing. 'Better late than never', is the famous adage. Even a late awakening will bring in some amount of happiness. Rather than crying over spilt milk, it is better to consider our self-fortunate for being still alive while some others are already dead and gone. If positivity, which is the happiness mantra, is adopted it can yet undo the mistakes done earlier. Even if one has- retired and the means of living have shrunk yet indulging in arts and hobbies can prove very useful. Ample time is available which should be utilized properly. The time spent in sleep is reduced and that saved time can be used for regular workout, yoga exercises, pranayam, swimming, believers can go to temples regularly and spend time in bhajan and kirtan. If you are living in a joint family, you can help by taking up small errands. You can spend time with your grandchildren chit chat with them, help in their studies, reach them to school and fetch them home. This will also help in passing time fruitfully. You will feel cheerful and the feeling that you can be of some help to someone will boost your positivity. All these measures are very important in ensuring good health.

Even those seniors who do not live in joint families, or if only the husband and wife stay together or live in the company of companions or in old age homes should follow a regular exercise regime. Along with practicing spiritualism, they should listen to music, read regularly, contact friends and relatives on phone in order to spend time fruitfully. They can also volunteer to render their services to some institutions related to senior citizens. This work may not be related to the vocation they followed all their life. Pet animals or birds can also be very endearing and they are able to reciprocate our feelings for them. The pets contribute by giving company to lonely people. In advanced age, we may not be able to achieve expertise in the fields of music, painting or photography but they can certainly engage our minds and give us joy. If we are physically fit, we can go to different places full of nature's bounty or go on holy pilgrimages to places of religious importance, which is another way of keeping ourselves happily busy.

When we make proper use of that wisdom which the school called 'life' teaches us, it is called 'experience'. We must make use of this wisdom and experience, not only for ourselves but for others too. The senior citizen's brain is a rich storehouse or library of knowledge. In underdeveloped tribes in countries like Africa, the elders' play an important role in giving justice and settling disputes because of their wisdom and experience. The reference books called senior citizens come in handy during such challenging situations.

If we pursue any positive activity it leads to profitable use of the time we have. Life gets new meaning and a new aim. Those people who do not have an aim are wasting away the time they have got because of increased longevity. They simply while away the time. We must discover our strengths, experience, and live accordingly. We need money to live life. Therefore, we must use the money we possess very carefully. We must remember that ruing the lack of money does not increase it nor can those seniors who have lots of money ensure happiness because of their possessions. We must decide to be contented in order to be happy.

It would be surprising to find that rich people are always happy. Scientists say that human brain is adaptive. Our brain decides that we must possess a certain thing and it is ready to slog in order to achieve it. Every young man y desires to have at least a million rupees in the bank account; a self owned flat, a four-wheeler. The moment when these wishes come true, he is extremely happy but his joy is short lived and momentary. The brain, which looks around, sees other richer people and starts comparing one's own assets with those who are still better off and decides new benchmarks of happiness. After those dreams are achieved then it turns towards Tata, Birla, Ambani and Bill Gates for comparison and finds that it is far behind. It grows sad once again. This is a never-ending story. We must know the limits of our achievement and be contended with what we have. This should be our aim. We must be contended with what we have but this does not mean that we should just be idle and not aspire for something better. Positive thoughts, spite less laughter and regular work out are the mantra of healthy long life. It is the key to blissful ageing.

One should wish for a long life but do not treat your body as a slave. It is a misconception that God is pleased with you when you make your body suffer. The body requires food, water and air. A happy and contended attitude and positivity are necessary as fertilizers for the mind. We must make use of the modern technology like smart phones, computers and internet. These gadgets help to stay connected with our relatives and friends as with the world at large. These gadgets can quench our thirst for new knowledge. Therefore, we must make every possible use of these equipments. This will help you to stay young at heart and reduce the monotony of life. We must always remember that 'variety is the spice of life.'

To be able to age gracefully is an achievement in itself. The genes have a major role to play in deciding our age. Even if they are unchangeable, the secret of achieving longevity is to inhale pure air, drink pure water, exercise regularly, accept, and respect the limits of one's physical and mental capacity.

Massage Therapy-

In recent times, the practice of visiting spas or massage parlors for getting whole body massage has increased among the young and old of the affluent classes in our society. Usually massage is taken as treatment in case of some injury or general weakness, for soothing the skin, muscles and bones and for de-stressing the whole body. Oil is applied to the entire body including the head and then it is massaged. Along with an expert masseur, a doctor's advice is also essential before we undergo this treatment. It is quite evident that massage as an external therapy existed hundreds of years ago and practiced by Ayurveda.

Childbirth involves risk to the life of two persons, the mother and the child. The mother has to go through intense labor pains. She not only gets physically tired while pushing the baby but also mentally exhausted because childbirth causes a lot of tension. The infant also undergoes tremendous mental and physical trauma while leaving the warmth and protection of the mother's womb and coming out into the open space.

Hence, in the Indian tradition the mother and the child are given an oil massage and a warm water bath daily for the next two months after childbirth. This is a very commendable practice.

If the injured muscles and points are massaged in a proper manner, they experience an early relief. The surface layer of dead skin is removed and the skin starts glowing radiantly and it appears pinkish in color. It gives the individual a more youthful appearance. The blood circulation around the muscles and joints is increased, tiredness is reduced and they feel more energetic. The entire body experiences a relaxed feeling. There is a lessening in the feeling of fatigue and this brings sound sleep. High blood pressure or hypertension can be brought under control and all the muscles are rejuvenated with the help of massage therapy.

Research conducted on massage revealed that massage increases the level of endorphin in the blood, which leads to lessening of pain. It also improves blood circulation because of which the cells of the muscles and skin are reproduced with renewed vigor. As stress, tension and weariness are reduced, the immunity level is also on the rise.

Massage has many advantages but we should not misunderstand it 'as a one shot medicine or a magic healer for all discomforts. It is necessary to seek the physician's advice for both the malady and the medicine. Massage can only be a supportive therapy not an alternative one.

The Rising Percentage of Senior Citizens

12

Huge trees and tortoises are known to live for ages. A hundred years ago, human longevity was very low. With the increased overall development in the field of medical science, the span of human life has extended considerably. Initially this was seen in the case of people living in advanced countries, which were financially as well as medically advanced. Now this is discernible even in developing countries also. This is also an age of fierce competition and the human being of today is engaged in a merciless rat race. This has given rise to materialism and easy methods of contraception have become available. People receive more sex education and consequently there is a reduction in birth rate. All these factors contribute to increasing the average human age. This obviously means that the number of aged is increasing as compared to that of the young and infants.

The young are an integral part of the work force of any nation. The senior citizens retire at the age of sixty. As they have become physically and mentally feeble and are more susceptible to illnesses; they cannot contribute in the development of the nation. In short, we can say that, the larger the number of young, efficient people in the country the possibility of achieving industrial development and economic growth is enhanced manifold. In contrast those nations which have a larger population of senior citizens may not progress much and are likely to fall behind. As the number of aged grows in the country, that becomes burdensome and has its ill effects on the economy of that nation. So those developed countries where the senior citizens were in a larger proportion, had to face all the problems which the aged experienced. The under developed or undeveloped countries faced the problems of increased longevity in recent times. This means that all the nations are battling with the enormous problem created because of the rising proportion of the aged in the society. As the span of life increases further, these problems will certainly take a gigantic form. The gravity of these issues was felt on an international level and so in the twentieth century the UNO felt the need to spread awareness about Ageing and hold discussions to find out solutions to handle the problem of human longevity. It was due to this concern that institutions such as Help the Aged, HelpAge, International, were established.

A person retires at the age of sixty. Different nations have different age limits for categorizing senior citizens but usually people ranging from sixty to sixty-five are considered as seniors. In 2010, the number of senior citizens all over the world was 524 million people. This was 8% of the total world population. It is estimated by experts that in 2050 this number will go up to 1.5 billion which will amount to 16% of the total population.

The population of India is around 1.25 billion and ranks the second largest in the world. The number of aged is around one billion. Experts estimate that by 2050, India will beat China in the population race and will become the country with the largest population of the aged, amounting to 1.6 billion. At present the aged amount to 8% of the total population in India. The percentage of the young is very large. Fifty percent of the population is above twenty-five years of age while sixty-five percent people are under the age of thirty-five years. Hence, from the international perspective India ranks the highest in terms of productive work force. This will lead India towards becoming an economic super power. Our Prime Minister is making all the necessary efforts to attract international investment for strengthening the 'Make in India' initiative. Namo namah!

Considering the increased longevity of the people, there is surely going to be a considerable growth in the number of the aged people. They will have to undoubtedly struggle against a number of problems such as economic, social, health related maladies and loneliness. If we consider the situation in the past few decades, we will realize that the tribulations caused due to ageing on the personal, social, national as well as international level need to be addressed carefully and solutions meticulously planned on a war footing.

Population Ageing- The meaning of population Ageing is that the majority population in all countries is growing older and older. There are two main reasons for this phenomenon. The first is the increased longevity due to the spectacular development made in the field of medicine and the second is the reduced rate of population growth. Gradually as the economic growth of any nation takes place, the above-mentioned causes are highlighted and the number of the aged people in the country grows. The reduced birth rate is also an important factor responsible for this. In the past, any number of children were accepted because children were considered as a gift from God. Later with more information and knowledge about the human reproduction and aids for birth control, they realized that children were not given to us by any God but was a manmade phenomenon. The realization of the ill effects of population explosion and that population control is all in our hands has led to initially a resolve such as,' we two, our two', being later revised to 'we two our only one' and finally to 'it is ok without children'. This has led to a relative rise in the percentage of the aged all over the world. This trend is termed as 'Population Ageing'. Those communities who fiercely defended their racial purity by vehemently refusing to give foreign emigrants citizenship are now inviting foreigners with open arms. According to the changed policies of such countries, they are now ready to encourage foreigners to become residents of their country. They are also promoting birth rate among citizens in their own country. As part of this strategy the government offers tax benefits to citizens with more children and concessions for educational and health purposes for children. Concessions and special offers are showered upon couples such as paternity and maternity leave for rearing their children is given to both the man and woman.

Population Ageing and National Economy:

There are some positive effects on the national economy due to population ageing. In developed countries, the elders have a large amount of savings and since the spending capacity of this age group is quite low the sale of consumer goods is also low. This reduces inflation and helps to keep interest rates low. Some economists are of the opinion that automated and technological advance receives a boost as the percentage of work force is reduced. The GDP of the nation may be lowered but because the aged have their savings, the percentage of economic stability and affluence is comparatively higher. This leads to less income through tax collection for the government. Therefore, it has to levy and increase VAT and other such taxes and has to reduce expenditure on health services and pension amounts or else the government's financial plans will go haywire. In order to control this slump the government will have to encourage those elders who are mentally and physically fit to continue to work for a longer span of time. It is also important to think about how this will have an adverse effect on youth employment and many young people will have to remain jobless.

In urban areas, both the husband and wife are engaged in their jobs. They require help for doing things such as buying vegetables or grocery, looking after the children, reaching them to school or sports classes, paying electricity and telephone bills on time, bank related work and so many other similar jobs. If the elders who are mentally fit offer to help by doing these jobs for their own or the neighbor's family they can spend their time fruitfully ,derive satisfaction for rendering help and also be able to earn a little. They can also work for charity or get an honorarium in institutions meant for helping the aged. This will make them feel significant, of some help to fellow aged people whose sufferings they can understand better, and help to soothe.

HelpAge India has begun this benevolent work on a very large scale. Similar institutions are active all over the world. These institutions help to improve the self-image among the aged and increase respect that the society gives them.

There are numerous problems caused due to ageing all over the world. It is essential to strike a balance between these problems and their solutions otherwise; we will have to face newer predicaments while trying to implement solutions for the old. It is indeed a tight ropewalk!

Senior Citizens and Law

Owing to the phenomenal progress in medical science, man's life expectancy has increased manifold. This was earlier possible in progressive countries but is now achievable even in developing countries. Generally, a person above the age of sixty is considered as old or senior citizen. In ancient times, there was no mechanism to note a person's birth date, year and age .It is only about three or four centuries ago that medical facilities became available. Prior to this era, there was no fixed definition of old age. When the person became weak and frail, was bent double and when his body became a storehouse of various diseases his close relatives would carry him to some remote valley or mountain, leave some food stock with him and leave him there, waiting to die. It was later that the elders started enjoying a position of deference in the family and they received financial and emotional support from the family members.

The number of elders is growing by the day. In 1951, there were two million old people in India. In 2001, this number rose to 7.2 million that was 8% of the total Indian population. By 2025, this number is estimated to rise up to 18% of the entire population.

Argentina raised the issue of senior citizens in the UNO for the first time. After that Malta which is a very small nation brought this subject on the anvil in 1969.So in 1971, the UNO General Assembly submitted a detailed report on this issue. In 1978, some rules and regulations were finalized, nationally as well as internationally on the issue of the aged. Therefore, in 1982, a global conference was arranged in Vienna from 26 July to 6 August on the topic of 'Ageing' and the 'Problems of Ageing'. The discussions held in the conference sought to find solutions regarding numerous issues related to the aged. Preparations began for finding solutions to problems of the aged, formulating an international definition of Ageing, deciding the nature of laws related to elders. Efforts to find measures to solve the financial, social, and mental and health related issues of the aged began in this conference.

The UNO prepared a five-point program regarding the rights of the aged on 16 December 1991. The program emphasized on the independence of the aged, care for the old, their respect in society and self-dependence. This gave the elders the opportunity to work and the choice to decide when to stop working, mix up in society, and participate in deciding the policies regarding their future as well as health care. They could learn new things; involve themselves in cultural, religious and entertainment programs and give them a position of respect and safety in the society. It was agreed that every government should take responsibility for the physical and mental security of the elders and prevent elder abuse.

First of October is celebrated as International Day of Older Persons. Let us now look at the laws related to the problems of the aged that exist in India.

Laws regarding Property:

Many people fail to decide how their property should be distributed after their death. Some make their will through some trust. They should properly plan it after understanding the existing laws with the help of legal experts. Many people start preparing their will after their brain and body refuse to work properly and they realize that the time to cross the bar is arriving soon. Many a times close relatives take undue advantage of the serious condition of the old person to prepare a will that is in their favor. They may even take signatures of the old person on blank papers. This is completely wrong. The person who prepares the will has to be mentally and physically fit and this has to be certified by a doctor.

Human life is transient. We are not sure when the curtains will be drawn over our life. Hence, it is prudent to prepare our will well in advance when we are in good health in young age or middle age. Later we can change the will any number of times if required. We must make it a point to register the will in the relevant office. If we wished to transfer our property, we were required to pay stamp duty but now the estate duty is cancelled.

We can mention our wish to donate our body organs in the will and our desire for euthanasia. It is important to submit the papers related to our will to the related office when we are in a healthy state of mind and body.

Health Insurance:

The health related ailments are already on the rise in case of the old people. They suffer from expensive maladies such as cataract, glaucoma, heart disease, prostate, cancer and joint replacement surgeries. Hospitalization is extremely expensive nowadays. Even medicines are very costly. They are more beneficial for the production companies rather than the patients. Hence it is necessary that we must be sufficiently insured for health related problems. We must be careful that we never skip paying the premium. The insurance companies are interested in finding out reasons to refuse to reimburse our expenses. So we must be careful about paying the premium regularly. We must inform the insurance company immediately in case of hospitalization, submit the insurance papers and cashless card to the hospital. We must be careful to submit all true information to the insurance company and the necessary medical reports. If we follow all these procedures correctly, there are a number of laws, which are beneficial for the old. Otherwise, instead of the rule of law what prevails is the rule of lucre.

Laws Related to Care Taking:

When illness such as dementia, paralysis or Alzheimer occurs in old age the person is unable to take any decisions and if he does, those decisions are not accepted by law. Hence, we should name a close relative before hand who could take care in case of an eventuality. We must also mention how much amount should be paid to the caretaker and all this should be registered with the relevant authorities. If we do not have, close relatives or we do not find them dependable we can choose anyone whom we are sure about as our caretaker.

Protection by Law:

The UNO Security Council has clearly specified international guidelines and stated principles about how to behave with the elders and the facilities that they should be given. Each country has adopted these principles but has made changes relevant to their conditions in finalizing their own policies and laws.

Indian Law:

Every region, state is given the freedom to decide the laws, allowances and facilities to be given to the elders according to their convenience. Though this is true the facilities and legal assistance that exists in our country has not received as much momentum as is evident in the developed countries.

As there is a lot of unemployment among the young, it is difficult to give jobs to the elders. Since the financial condition is poor, we lack in making provisions such as homes for the aged, pension to those working in unorganized sectors and health care. It is not possible for the aged to stand for their rights because they cannot afford going to court, appointing lawyers and waiting endlessly for the long drawn legal process to end after which they may get the facilities. Thus, they are left to the mercy of God and destined to die, without enjoying their rights.

According to the Hindu Law and Muslim Personal Law the son, daughter or inheritor should take care of the elders, provide them food, clothing, shelter, take care, and provide proper medical aid when they are sick. If this does not happen out of a sense of affection and duty towards the old, how far can legal provisions help? It is the government's policy to teach children to take up these responsibilities and make them aware of the legal facilities in their student age itself. The Muslim Personal Law includes the grandchildren also in the people who should take responsibility of the aged.

Since there are no separate Christian and Parsi Laws the children or successors in Christian and Parsi families can be prosecuted if they do not take responsibility of the elders under Criminal Procedure Code. A large number of Indians live in villages. They hardly earn enough to feed their family, which consists of the husband wife and children. In such cases, looking after the elders becomes even more complicated. The young cannot do anything even if they wish to. The elders have no other alternative but to depend upon the government policies and facilities.

The responsibility of the Government:

1) a) Pension scheme to be implemented for the aged working in the unorganized sector

    b) Government should give donations for old homes or establish old homes one each for two to three districts

    c) Employment bureau for citizens above sixty years of age

    d) 30 to 50 % concession in bus, train and air travel

    e) Free health care facilities for the aged in all government hospitals.

2) Age- well foundations should seek advice from elders while preparing policies for the welfare of the elders.

3) School students should be taught to take responsibility of the elders and be made aware of their responsibilities and duties towards the old.

4) The elders should be granted their pension, provident fund and gratuity amounts as soon as possible.

5) The health related problems of the aged should be given preference.

6) Income tax concessions to earning elders

7) Schemes such as Jeevan Dhara, Jeevan Akshay Yojana, Senior Citizen Unit Yojana and Health Insurance should be implemented by the LIC.

8) Seniors should be given ten kilos of grains every month under the Vajpayee Annapurna scheme.

9) Ten percent of the houses built in the rural as well as urban areas should be reserved for the elders. Affordable home

loan schemes should be developed. These homes should be aged- friendly such as : they must have stair cases with railings fitted but ideally these homes should be situated on the ground floor.

Rather than discussing how good these facilities are it is important to find out how stringent laws can be made in order to provide these facilities immediately and effectively to the aged. The reason for the lacuna in this system is lack of political will to implement the laws efficiently.

The state governments are expected to enforce the law passed in 2007 regarding the daily needs of the aged. According to this act, parent means natural or adopted, real or step father and mother. If the children refuse to look after their parents then these senior citizens can appoint a person or institution, give them the power of attorney and get the facilities meant for them. Most seniors are not physically and mentally able to pursue their demands, go to court for them. In such circumstances, the power of attorney holder helps them in all their efforts. If the senior citizen has made an appeal in the court for alimony, the court is vigilant in getting the children to pay them interim maintenance. Even childless senior citizens can legally demand such assistance from their successors. There is provision in the law for retrieving the estate or home or other property previously gifted to someone.

The demand to include the senior citizens' right to food, clothing, shelter and health care service in the list of fundamental rights is gaining momentum and support.

The joint family system is fast crumbling; emotional ties are no longer as strong as they were in the past, materialism and growing self-centeredness of the present generation makes it impossible for the seniors to live with self-respect. Though the government is passing favorable laws, they are not being strongly implemented and so some others are benefitted instead of the aged.

We all know that laws are made to regulate social life. In the same way, the elders should be aware of the laws made in order to ensure that their physical, financial, social and mental life is tolerable and peaceful. Laws made for the seniors should be considered as important as their support, their 'walking stick'.

Elder Abuse: Exploitation, Humiliation & Hurt

Along with many advantages of ageing, we have started experiencing some disadvantages also. A sizeable bank of wise, experienced and matured old people started accumulating in the society, which enriches not only the family but also the society, nation and the world at large. We can see a large number of senior citizens around us who are stalwarts in the field of literature, various arts, social work, scientific research, politics and many other faculties. Scientists and other experts who have accomplished exemplary success in their field of work are honored with Nobel prizes every year. It can be easily seen that most of the awardees are senior citizens.

The new generation is also finding new paths and giving the society new directions for progress. The young have achieved a lot of advancement in the field of industry. Nevertheless, the number of senior citizens is larger in the areas of literature and arts, some are politicians who decide national and international relations and diplomacy. If you consider the world population of the aged then the proportion of seniors who are working at the top ranks and are instrumental in navigating the society is very minuscule. A large number of old people have to helplessly lead a neglected life full of hardships. On the one hand, while the society profits due to the experience which the aged can share, on the other hand they have to confront a rising avalanche of problems related to family, society, finance, mental and physical health. Ageing reduces the physical capacity of the people. They suffer from depression due to lack of physical and mental strength, reduced income and a number of diseases. Sometimes they are dependent on others due to physical debility. This results in reducing their self-esteem and self-evaluation. It also damages their self-respect and results in depression.

In the present age of fierce competition, the new generation has to face innumerable conflicts. The husband and the wife both are required to earn for a living. We can see that as religious and moral values are declining very fast, materialism and avarice have proliferated in the society. Hence gone are the days when the senior citizens could depend upon the younger generation for a peaceful and happy old age. The old have started feeling cast away and neglected by the family and society. As if this were not enough, there are numerous instances, in which the old have to face physical and mental torture. This persecution of elders has been internationally termed as 'Elder Abuse'. Even if the UNO has defined this harassment of the old, words are not enough to describe the maltreatment these elders have to go through.

If those relatives, about whom the elders feel confident and expect support, disappoint them through action or ignore them repeatedly or even once causing pain to the elders it is termed as 'torture'.

Suffering could be of various types such as physical, mental, emotional or financial affliction. Even not maintaining cleanliness of the dependent and physically disabled person can be categorized as misery.

The International Senior Centre organized an Asia Pacific Round Table Conference in the city of Pune in India in the year 2006.The theme of the conference was 'Elder Abuse'. Every individual has the right to live a life free of fear and suffering. No one should exploit, ignore or disrespect them. Accepting that no one has the right to make the elders feel insignificant is a characteristic feature of being human. There has to be a distinction between the human beings and animals. While differentiating between man and animals we must also realize the distinction between torture of the aged and the crimes committed against them. The criminal offences are dealt with by the police and court whereas the responsibility of hardships of the elders lies jointly upon the family, relatives, society and government. The suffering of the old is a very sensitive issue. Most often, the relatives torture the elders against whom they dare not speak. They feel humiliated to mention that their own family members are inflicting pain and they are afraid of the anger and revengefulness that might cause. This agony is disturbing and painful for the elders. They are afraid of being accused of losing their wits and being turned out of the house.

Some of them feel that pain is inflicted upon them as their wife and children wish to take revenge for their behavior in the past. They hold their stars responsible for the pain and live with the feeling of guilt. They suffer silently because most of them do not even know where they should lodge a complaint against this ill treatment. Hence, they can get no justice.

Dr. Sharadchandra Gokhale has rendered yeoman service, in the field related to solving the problems of the aged on an international level. He opines that the reasons behind the ill treatment of the old are- general ignorance in the society regarding the rights of the aged, the absence of the urge for independence among the old, the responsibility of the family to look after the elders which is a part of our culture and the lack of a sense of social responsibility. Attention is being paid on an international level to the afflictions on the elders, domestic violence, health related issues and crimes against the aged. The increasing urbanization in developing countries, industrialization is also responsible for increasing the suffering of the elders. The persecution of elders is on the rise in families, society and institutions. Scarcity of space and money is experienced especially by the rural aged. The condition of those living under the poverty line and belonging to the backward castes in our society is very pitiful. Among these, women are the ones who are the most neglected.

The 2006 Asia Pacific Round Table Conference suggested a number of policies and laws in order to curb the cruelty and crimes against the old. It also suggested that records should be maintained in case of such brutal behavior against the old. It also made a public appeal to all media to give proper coverage to incidents of elder abuse. It is our prime duty to spread awareness among the people regarding the fact that everyone has a right to an exploitation free and fearless existence. The media should make efforts to spread this understanding in the society. Similarly social welfare institutions should also take an initiative in awakening the people. It was also suggested that systems should be established to give legal advice and extend emotional support and counseling to victims of such abuse as well as develop measures to avoid elder abuse.

In the inaugural session of this round table conference Tina Ambani of Reliance Group addressed the elders as 'citizens of silver age' and expressed her wish to see them treasured and empowered all over the country. The young do not appreciate that the old face many problems related to health, finance, wholesome food and emotional well being as well as certain nagging issues, which they are unable to express. The young may understand it when they grow old but till then it will be very late for the elders. This indifference among the young causes loss of self-respect and confidence for the aged.

What the Round Table of 2006 accomplished? :

While preparing a definition of elder abuse, the conference included physical, emotional, mental, sexual and financial exploitation of the elders. It also included the ill treatment of the old occurring due to consciously or unconsciously ignoring them.

The Round Table Conference accepted the following points:

1) Elder abuse should not be tolerated.

2) Every citizen has the right to live a fearless and respectable life free from terror and oppression.

3) Every individual has the right to take decisions regarding one's own life.

4) In the case of people who, owing to illness or accident, have lost the capacity to make decisions regarding their own life and illness other people or institutions may decide on their behalf. While doing so they must keep in mind the welfare of the persons and the viewpoint , which he or she may have expressed earlier and the customs and traditions of the culture to which the persons belong.

The following findings were noted in the Conference brochure.

1) It was accepted that elder abuse does take place.

2) The elders suffer devaluation because of this abuse.

3) Appropriate policies and laws should be made in order to give the old legal protection from abuse.

4) The society, media, institutions which provide support service and government should help to spread awareness regarding elder abuse.

5) In order to encourage elders to speak about the abuse they go through, it is necessary to formulate a policy to empower them.

6) Prepare a database regarding records of elder abuse.

7) To prepare with the help of legislative measures a list of rules and regulations for senior women who are dependent on their children or those who are unable to decide for themselves

8) To pursue cases of elder abuse and publicize them with the help of media

9) To make it mandatory for all institutions in service of the aged to follow certain minimum quality standards

10) To strengthen grievance redress cells and counseling centers for the aged

11) To organize programs for reconciling and reinforcing the mutual relations between the two generations

12) UNO and the governments of member countries should implement the policies immediately

To provide helpline for the aged

To create institutions for elder care

To establish counseling centers and facilitation centers

To make the process of procuring pension hassle free

To increase communication among institutions for the aged with a view to reducing the loneliness of the old

To establish a rapport between nursing and health care institutions with social institutions for establishing communication between the tortured and the torturers as also to increase awareness among the old about their rights and duties

To make relevant changes from time to time in the laws meant for the old

To conduct continuous research regarding he problems and suffering of the aged

The suggestions made by Dr. Shiv Raju have been implemented at present.

With a view to be able to consider all the aspects of elder abuse, it is necessary to define it carefully, to find precautionary measures, support and train care givers , to determine the duties and responsibilities of the family, society, institutions and to provide them with guidelines and legal knowhow.

In 2002 WHO, the international health organization conducted a research on elder abuse entitled, 'Missing Voices', in which it noted that,"self respect and reverence are as important to humans as food and water."

Reasons for elder abuse

While discussing the issues related to elder abuse gerontologists trace its origin to social factors and not legal ones. Sociologists feel that social changes are responsible for elder abuse and criminologists call this a crime committed by the younger generation. Social workers emphasize upon the importance of empowering the aged and rendering service and medical facilities to them. Medical science feels that proper medical treatment and care should be given while psychologists depend upon counseling and therapy to solve the problems of the old.

It is essential to bring about a reformation in the society by creating awareness on this issue. Young children should be made aware of their responsibility towards solving the problems of the aged through school education itself. All kinds of media also can contribute effectively in educating the children. Media renders a major role in determining and shaping social psyche. Even information bureaus can actively participate in these efforts. Nonprofit institutions can also contribute a lot.

Policy of the Indian Government:

While deciding policy for addressing elder abuse it is noticed that though taking care of the old is the responsibility of the family members, there are numerous reasons why the elders cannot depend on them. This situation has arisen in India because the life span of Indians has gradually increased over the years along with rising inflation.

The Indian policy focuses on, at least providing financial support to the elders for health services, food, clothing and shelter. It also specifies special aid for women. The senior citizens can make use of help lines to seek assistance. They can remain in touch with their relatives and friends. They can also contact hospitals .This facility is usually provided through nonprofit institutions.

Senior citizens become victims of criminal activities quite easily. They can be cheated and mentally and physically tortured. Bearing in mind the possibility that their own family members can dupe the elders or threaten them and take away their property the policy has carefully considered measures to protect the aged and punish the criminals. These services are provided by nonprofit organizations and the police department is directed to keep a friendly vigil on the aged.

The Indian constitution assures every citizen the right to life and individual liberty. The policy has made provisions for giving additional security to the elderly if necessary. Legal provision is made for elders to claim maintenance from their son or daughter.

In 2009, Dr.Shiv Raju has made certain suggestions on this topic to the Government of India. It is necessary to examine elder abuse from a social point of view and counsel both the old person who is a victim and the victimizer.

Causes for the ill treatment of elders should be analyzed and abuse evaluated.

Today elder abuse has become a very complicated problem. It is ubiquitous and is found in all countries, castes, classes, prince and pauper alike. Since the family maintains confidentiality in such issues, very little of it is discussed openly. That is the reason why we cannot fully understand the gravity of the problem. The financially weak old people do not have the resources to satisfy even their daily needs whereas the rich are emotionally starved. The aged women suffer in a larger measure. According to Tina Ambani, it is necessary for the family, neighborhood and society to make sincere efforts towards improving the condition of the elders. Those who are young now must keep in mind that they too will become old after some years and so must avoid ill-treating them. Their children watch them and learn through imitation about how to treat the elders. The government also should take firm steps to handle this problem. In fact, people from all lifestyles should actively participate in this mission against elder abuse.

Evening Shadows

15

The journey of life is both weird and wonderful. The wolf's story in Aesop's fables is very enlightening. The wolf that goes to the jungle for catching a prey sees his own long shadow in the early hours of the morning and is elated. He feels he has been able to create the impression that he is enormous in size. He decides to kill a gigantic elephant. Since he has decided upon finding an elephant as his prey he ignores smaller animals and walks past them. As time passes his shadow starts shrinking in size and by midday it is so tiny that it is almost under his feet. He realizes that actually he is very small. A small prey would have been sufficient for him. Tormented with hunger he decides that now even a tiny mouse would suffice to satisfy his hunger.

Childhood is a period of narrow perception and a very limited world while youth is a phase of overriding confidence. The wishes and ambitions are like fast galloping horses. The sky is the limit for them. Youth is the era of watching dreams and working day in and day out to fulfill them. They are ready to go to any extent to provide whatever is the best for their children. Just as the heat of the sun grows to its maximum capacity by midday in the same way in middle age the brunt of reality around an individual becomes acute. The physical energy also starts waning. The individual becomes more considerate and perceptive. The difference between dream and reality becomes evident. The wings that aspired to scale great heights become weak and the need to have a strong foothold on the ground becomes a priority. By the evening of life both the physical enthusiasm and mental strength is reduced. The person starts craving for rest and harmony. Every individual passes through these phases of dawn, morning, midday, evening in one's life.

By the time we reach the evening of our life we start giving it sweet names like 'seniority' and 'maturity' but the young often ridicule the people in this phase as 'old hag', 'old bag', 'codger' or 'coot'. During the evening of life, a person has grown insightful through experience. Astuteness acquired through experience cannot be purchased with money, intelligence or education. Wisdom is achieved only after experiencing life that means walking through life and braving its storms and upheavals. Someone else's experience cannot help us to understand life; we have to experience it ourselves. Intelligence is an innate gift and is based on genetic factors while experience has to be earned through actually living life, which comes in handy when we advise the next generation.

It is up to the young whether to consider the aged as dustbins and put them aside, ignore them saying that they have become senile, or to enrich oneself out of their experience and use their wisdom profitably. The aged must also keep in mind that on the background of change in the times a number of other things also change simultaneously and so they must try to change their choices and preferences accordingly. They make their life as well as the young people's life miserable if they continue to insist on their own point of view. In old age owing to high blood pressure, diabetes, atherosclerosis the blood supply to the brain is reduced. Hence the old people repeat what they have already said innumerable times. The youngsters should understand this and should not get irritated by the repetition. They should just ignore it. They should also consider the fact that the old are prone to forgetfulness. If both, the old and the young understand these physical and mental changes and limitations of the old only then can they deal with each other patiently. If this happens then the old generation and the new, the experienced and the inexperienced, young and seniors can live together in harmony and unity. They will get a strong base to live together. This is beneficial for both the generations.

If we expect the young to yearn for the old, the old must understand the problems faced by the youth. Rather than criticizing the views, style of living, eating, drinking and sleeping habits of the young the old must accept the behavior that is suited to their times. They must only be alert that the young are not getting addicted to habits that would physically, financially, mentally and socially ruin them. There is no harm in sharing one's opinion about financial matters such as investments but the decision should be left to the young so that they will be responsible for the consequences such as profit or loss. The grand parents should certainly pamper the grand children but they must also be supportive of the young parents when they are stern while disciplining them in their studies, regular exercises and developing good habits. It is not proper for the elders to crib about their illness as soon as the son or daughter in law return tired from work. Nevertheless, they should certainly inform the young about their maladies well in time before the situation aggravates further. If the seniors have arranged for their financial needs after retirement, they should not burden the young with demands for money.

If the daughter in law is a working person, the mother in law should help her in looking after the grandchildren, their studies, play and the daily domestic chores. While the son is struggling to win success in the prime of his youth the father can manage to run small errands outside for paying electricity and phone bills, connecting with relatives, reaching the grand children to their school, class and play. Now the young also can do the job of paying bills through net banking. If the two generations consider each other's comfort then it is possible for the old to live happily. If each one decides to make certain compromises at every stage in life it would be possible to say 'bon voyage' rather than feel terrified by the lengthening shadows of life.

Not all seniors can live in this manner in their families. Around fifty years ago joint family system prevailed as an integral part of our culture. Nowadays even if there is an affectionate bond between the old generation and the new, it is not possible for them to stay together. There could be a number of problems like limited space, financial crunch, jobs in remote or far off areas, or foreign countries because of which the aged and the young have to live in separate households. Few alternatives have now become available for facing such situations.

If the elders are required to move out of the city or town in which they have spent a major part of their life, they do not know how to spend their time in the new, unfamiliar place because they hardly know anyone there. The young who have migrated to the urban areas because of their jobs have to adjust in small houses and small earnings. They cannot keep the elders with them even if they wish to for want of space. Children who opt for better earning opportunities and settle abroad are comparatively better off but elders may not feel at home in the foreign country or the climate may not be suitable for them. Therefore, even if their mutual relations are warm the seniors cannot live together with the youngsters. Consequently, both the generations have to live separately. The seniors may have their own house to stay. When one of the partners is no more the other partner is left all alone. When both are together, it is beneficial because they can share their joys and sorrows and can take care of each other when ill. A single person misses all these advantages. The only alternative left for such single senior citizens are homes for the aged.

It is worthwhile to visit the old home managed by Loksewa Foundation at Khanapur as it is a model home for the aged. We must appreciate what Dr. Vinod Shah, the pillar of strength for this old home has to say. More information about HelpAge India, Paranjpe Schemes' Athashree Projects will follow in the subsequent chapters, which could prove helpful to those who require such services.

HelpAge India

16

Till recently the joint family system was in vogue in India and some other underdeveloped countries and the life expectancy rate was also very low. As a result the problems of the aged were also very less. Human life expectancy increased with improved economic development, education and health care services. As a result, the problems of the aged developed suddenly. The need to solve the problems, plan accordingly, find solutions, and implement them immediately became the major concern of the people. England and Japan were the first to start with planning and making provisions to solve these tribulations.

Support for the Aged

Cecil Jackson Cole who founded the international organization for the old, HelpAge International visited India in 1974. He invited Mr. Samson Daniel who resided in India to England to give him a three months training in how to collect charity for the cause of the aged. After returning from this training Daniel and his wife, both decided that service for the old was to be their life mission. The international senior citizen's institution, HelpAge International recruited more staff to cover Bombay, Madras and Calcutta in 1975. Ninety seven countries including India were involved in finding out solutions for the problems of the aged. Representatives of all the ninety-seven nations participated in these efforts made by the international organization viz., the UNO. HelpAge India an institution, which worked for the senior citizens, also became a member of the international institution dedicated for elder care. Even today this institution is affiliated to the institution in England and the UNO has appreciated the exemplary work it has accomplished. This Indian institution for the elders situated in Delhi has been registered and approved as an institution. This institution became financially independent in a matter of three months. The donations made towards this institution can claim income tax exemptions according to 12 A and 80 G.

HelpAge India is a non-political, non-profit, secular, non-government and autonomous organization. This is an organization registered according to the Registration Act and works on the national level.

HelpAge India is a non-profit organization, which helps more than a crore elders in India. The present generation of senior citizens were so preoccupied with the welfare of their families that they had not imagined the kind of problems they would be required to face after their energetic youth had faded away. They feel dejected because they do not receive warmth and care from the family as well as the society. They feel sad for being disregarded. They had not anticipated in their younger days that the changes in economic, social and family values would affect them so ruthlessly. They were unprepared for the changed reality of the present times. Nevertheless, they have to resign to the situation. Old age is accompanied by debility and sickness, unbearable loneliness owing to the death of the partner. These reasons are enough to trigger depression in the old.

Many non-profit institutions are doing commendable work in trying to find out solutions for the problems of the aged. HelpAge India is running an excellent and very well planned holistic program for the aged. This organization was established in 1978.This institution is also trying to strongly present the problems of the old before the government. As a result, the Indian Government is finalizing a policy, which is beneficial for the elders. It is rendering outstanding service in the areas of providing the aged means of livelihood, shelter and health care in twenty-three urban and rural regions in India. HelpAge India seeks the cooperation of individuals, institutions and government in fulfilling its mission.

The major objective of this organization is to help all the needy senior citizens and serve them well.

The motto of HelpAge India is to provide the elderly the right to active, healthy and dignified life. It is with this objective in mind that their programs are planned and executed. These should not only solve the present day problems but also consider the problems likely to occur in the future. The planning has to be long term in view of all the possible tribulations the old are likely to face. At present health insurance, pension for all and facilities suited to age have been made available. The organization is aware of the fact that compared to the scope and measure of the problems faced by the aged that is enormously large the work done all over the world to ameliorate these problems is very small.

HelpAge India has decided its objectives for 2020.

They hope to achieve the following milestones by the Year 2020:

1) Livelihood security with all available amenities for two million elderly through institutions of elderly

2) Health security for two million elderly

3) Give them a voice with political support

4) To provide age appropriate services to 12 million elderly in partnership with government, private sector and civil society

5) To prepare the aged to live a life and future with self respect and esteem

HelpAge India helps seniors to exercise their rights, to stop violence against them, to assist needy seniors in obtaining reverse mortgage and to establish senior citizen clubs in order to lessen their loneliness. It also helps in getting them health insurance, maintenance from their children and seeing that the government allocates a budgetary allowance for the aged. It also gives suggestions to the government in preparing policies for the benefit of the aged. HelpAge India renders valuable service to the cause of the aged by providing health care, security, shelter and helping them in times of natural calamities.

HelpAge India receives help from patrons, institutions, industrialists, companies and trusts. Even international organizations such as European Union, Emergency Services Institute, International Development Institution and Japan Foundation are keen to support HelpAge India.

Projects by HelpAge India

1   Mobile Health Care

These vans deliver health care to the doorstep of disabled seniors. It is as if an ambulance is equipped with a mobile hospital, an M.B.B.S. doctor, a pharmacist, a social worker and a driver. This van has a stock of the best medicines and visits various parts of the city or village every day at a particular time between 9 am and 5pm. It renders free medical consultation and medicine to the old. As the day and time of the arrival of this van is fixed, the aged gather even before it arrives. Obviously while they wait for the van to arrive they chit chat and share their problems with one another. They feel relaxed and happy. Around 1.7 million aged are benefitted every year. There are 97 mobile health care units for this purpose which cover over 20 regions and 1085 social sites. This is the largest mobile medical project in the whole of Asia.

2   Prevention of Blindness

If the aged are operated for cataract, they can live their life independently. They can earn their living again and live with self-respect. HelpAge India also provides patients in the last stages of cancer or other fatal diseases palliative care and freedom from pain.

The number of blind in India is very dismal.81percentage of the population suffers blindness due to cataract and every year we have an addition of two million people. In India, the proportion of ophthalmologists to the population is merely 1:1 lakh. It is a very benevolent task to help in getting cataract surgeries done. With the initiative taken by HelpAge India, 8.5 lakh cataract surgeries have been performed until date. Many organizations should come forward to contribute in this 'prevent blindness' drive.

3   Physiotherapy, Physio Care

Along with old age comes joint pain, waist pain, paralysis which obstructs free movements and makes the person dependent on others. HelpAge India helps such seniors by reducing their pain and making them as self reliant as possible. It renders this service every year to 10375 elders in 22 regions in India.

4   Support a Gran

Support a Gran is a scheme in which the wealthy people adopt the poor aged people and look after them. In 2013-14 in this program called 'Helping the Grandfather' 45237 rural, destitute seniors were given food, clothing and shelter. Those patrons and institutions who contribute to such projects are absolutely worth saluting!

5   Self Help

HelpAge India has helped 5300 urban and rural aged from 17 states to become self reliant by providing them money in order to start self-employment projects.

6   Elder Helpline 1800-180-1253

This service is available in the capital cities of twenty states. Under this scheme if those seniors who have to suffer violence, are turned out of the house or are tortured can contact the help line that is toll free. They can get assistance immediately. Government officers, police and other authorities are contacted by HelpAge India to seek assistance from them for helping the aged.

7   Cancer

Cancer is a dreaded word and the mere mention gives any one jitters. It is closely associated with old age. If cancer is detected in the early stages of the disease, the treatment is less expensive and consumes less time. HelpAge India organizes cancer detection camps for the benefit of the aged. So far 25000 aged have been examined and treatment for more than 10000 patients arranged by HelpAge India. The treatment for cancer, surgery and medicines are very expensive. HelpAge India has collected 6.5 crore rupees for meeting the expenses so far.

8   Day Care Center and Old Age Homes

Food, clothing and shelter are man's basic needs. Young people have the capacity of fulfilling them in any which way. The aged may not be able to satisfy these needs because of financial or physical impediments. In order to provide these basic needs HelpAge India renders financial assistance as well as guidance to day care centers or old homes. HelpAge runs old homes in Kadlur (Pondicherry) and Kolkata and helps other 194 old homes in different ways.

9   Disaster Care

The aged suffer a lot when disasters such as earthquakes, volcanic eruptions, tsunami, incessant rain and floods occur. HelpAge India rushes to their rescue during such calamities.

10   Livelihood Support

Those senior citizens who are physically and mentally fit but do not have any source of income are supplied with some money as capital for investing in small businesses so that they can earn their living. They can then live with self-respect. HelpAge India helps in providing such opportunities to the aged.3200 groups in India have assisted 42000 senior citizens to live a respectable life.

11   Tamraikulam Elders Village

On the Cuddalore –Puttucheri road in Tamaraikulam an ideal rehabilitation center has been established with the help of NDTV viewers. After the 2004 tsunami, 100 senior citizens who were rendered destitute were housed in this center. HelpAge India started it as a model center. It fulfills all the needs of the inmates such as health care, provides means for livelihood, and offers entertainment and shelter.

12   Educational Programs

If discipline regarding all facets of life, may be personal and social hygiene or even traffic rules is imbibed in the childhood itself it is easily practised all through one's life. HelpAge India keeps this principle in mind when it guides young school and college children about respecting the old, helping them in times of difficulty and giving them company in their loneliness. When these young children are suggestively made aware of the fact that they too would become old and face similar problems the disparity in the points of view of the two generations is reduced. This project is highly praiseworthy because it reduces differences helps to build between them a bridge of affection.

13   Government Support

HelpAge India is watchful in creating awareness among the administrative machinery that the government decides rules and regulations, designs and implements policies for the institutions, which render old age care, and makes budgetary provisions for the problems of the elders. It also sees to it that the legal provision that compels relatives to pay elders maintenance is strictly implemented and the aged are provided legal security. Because of the work done by HelpAge India, all seniors are provided pension, health care, awareness and a sense of responsibility is created by including educational inputs in school texts regarding service to the aged and legal provisions available.

HelpAge India supports and encourages elders by conducting such projects which inspire the elders to lead an active life.

14   Associations of the Aged

HelpAge India works for setting up institutions, which cater to the various needs of the aged, and conducts projects to guide these institutions. It follows the dictum, 'To motivate others to do social work is the greatest social work!' It also organizes entertainment programs, get together programs and excursions for the aged.

15   Project Advantage Card

Just as we use credit and debit cards, malls often issue their own advantage cards that offer their customers certain concessions.

HelpAge India issues Advantage Cards to senior citizens above the age of sixty. They can avail of 10% to 20% reduction in prices on commodities or services with the help of this card when they visit clinics, diagnostic centers, hospitals, undergo surgery. They can use it even when they shop for daily necessities. This is indeed a boon to those elders who are financially weak. Even those senior citizens who are well off and pay income tax receive some tax reduction benefit by the government.

HelpAge India's efforts to find solutions to the problems faced by the aged are highly laudable. The organization has been highly appreciated nationally as well as internationally. It has received a number of prizes such as Bharat Nirman Prize, Times of India Award, and Award for financial discipline, Award for giving ideal health care. The best award that is above all these awards is the benedictions of all aged from all walks of life which HelpAge India receives.

HelpAge website: www.helpageindia.org
Contact: Manager Rajeev Kulkarni
Pune Office Contact no. 020-20265513
Mobile: 94422020699

15 June 2016, was internationally designated as World Elder Abuse Awareness Day. The 'Save our Seniors', (SOS)', an Android application was launched by HelpAge India, to mark this occasion. We can download this application from Google Play Store on any android phone. This will help senior citizens to get assistance in difficulties very easily. Topics related to senior citizens such as health, financial planning, abuse and exploitation of the aged, dynamic while ageing, will legacies, right entitlements will be available.

It will also be possible to get information regarding all the facilities available to members and cardholders of HelpAge India. The most important feature is that if in an emergency the 'sos' call helpline button is pressed the caller will be connected to State HelpAge, India, helpline.

Age Well Foundation is one of the leading institutions from among the numerous institutions, which work for solving the problems of the aged. Here are a few more details about the work done by Age Well Foundation.

Happy Ageing Foundation is a global institution. This institution has taken the initiative of serving the aged, especially the destitute. The main office of Happy Ageing Foundation situated in Delhi was first begun in 1999. When we contacted the President of this institution, Mr. Himanshu Rath, he gave us complete information about the working of Age Well.

One hundred and fifty charitable institutions work under the aegis of Age Well Foundation. They are spread over an expanse of six hundred and forty districts. In this institution, volunteers work in a two-tier system. At the primary level, they have seven thousand five hundred and eighty thousand volunteers work under their guidance. The first rung of volunteers comprises retired IAS officers and educated people from well-to-do background. All of them jointly provide service to almost thirty five thousand elders while supplying the senior citizens with various services. They have also established an employment exchange to provide full time or part time job opportunities to the elderly. They provide health care training, to the senior citizens. They also provide various equipments, which are useful for the disabled elders. They alert the police regarding security and other problems faced by the senior citizens. The destitute elders are provided with food grains. Age Well serves the cause of elders in a multi-faceted manner. A large number of study groups undertake responsibility of observing and collecting data regarding the problems faced by the elderly.

The service rendered by this institution has received international acclaim. Age Well has been conferred the title COSOC-universal counsel and has been granted consultative status.

Contact: **Shri Himanshu Rath,**
Chairman
Age Well Foundation, C-8 Lajpat Nagar, Second Floor

Extended Family

17

It is unfortunate that the joint family system has crumbled down and given way to single families. Nevertheless, the onset of the night does not mean that darkness has come to stay! The sun is going to rise and there is going to be light. Just as the new day dawns after the dark night there are new rays of hope in the form of the rise of the concept of extended families.

All relations are burdened with expectations the moment they are born. As we move around with this yoke, we experience disappointment and strained relations. Once the minds are separated, they can never be united. If one is compelled to stay on in such stressed circumstances, it leads to tension and despair. This gives rise to a feeling of enmity, which leads on to tolerating affliction, or even committing suicide. With the dawn of the new day, new hope arises. The new light gives opportunities for searching new alternatives. According to the popular saying, 'Necessity is the mother of invention,' new relations are established and one can become a member of an extended family in the form of institutions like 'Athashri' or old age homes. These relations may not be affectionate like blood relations. Even in blood relations, the elders experience that the warmth is already missing. However, this extended family consists of a large number of members. They do not have any expectations from one another and hence there is no disenchantment and the resultant stress and tension or dejection. If we do not get along with one person, there are others. One can choose from a number of people with whom to acquaint one's self.

They can come together, arrange programs for entertainment, exercise, stroll around, and have their breakfast, lunch, dinner alone or in the company of the inmates. They can choose being alone or being in company as they wish. Their children and grandchildren can come, meet them if their relationship is one of affection, and stay in the guest quarters for a few days. They can stay together without any burden of expectations from anyone.

Athashri Society

We visited Paranjpe scheme's extended family situated in Bawdhan and Pashan in Pune to know more about these projects. The first Athashri Sankul situated on Pashan-Sus road began in 1999. It was far away from the crowded city, in an area blessed with natural beauty. There was not even a grocery shop in the vicinity so the sankul even ran grocery shops. When you enter the premises of Athashri you will see wide roads, parking lots and pleasant greenery with innumerable trees and flowers. There is a gymnasium and a swimming pool in the premises. A small open-air theatre and a cinema screen are available for entertainment. There is a small temple for the devout inmates. Those seniors who wish to do some gardening are welcome to water the plants. Those who have their own vehicle may drive to the city everyday if they wish to. Those that don't could avail of the bus service available at Athashri. It is astonishing to see how while designing the building the requirements of the seniors at their age, their problems, their physical capacity and weaknesses have been taken into consideration in its minutest details. Most of the apartments have a drawing hall, a kitchen and a bedroom, are easy to maintain, and reasonably priced. The toilets are equipped with commodes to facilitate elders who suffer from knee joint problems. Old people are prone to slip and fall over wet areas. Their activities are hampered because of debility. In order to avoid this possibility, bars are fitted all over so that they get support while moving. The toilet doors slide with ease. The hassle of lifting and connecting gas cylinders is avoided because cooking gas is supplied to the kitchens through pipe lines. Facilities such as furniture, wardrobe are provided in the bedroom and drawing hall. A call bell is placed close to the bed and is easily accessible in case the person requires help.

As you enter the building, you come to the entrance lobby. You will meet the manager and his staff who are constantly at their work. Comfortable seating is provided in the lobby for visitors. The seating is slightly elevated so that the seniors can sit there at ease. There are very few steps and stairs. Slopes have been supplied where necessary and they are kept slightly coarse to avoid slipping. Passenger and stretcher elevators are fitted along with the staircases for reaching all the upper floors. In order to make it convenient for the elders to use the staircases the distance between two steps is one and a half inches lesser than the usual height. A long broad passage runs in the middle. This passage is useful during rains and in scorching sunlight for the elders to move around. Bars are fitted everywhere for support. There are chairs and small tables fitted at intervals along the passage for the elders to rest .There are covered sit-outs for them to sit, in groups and watch the garden below.

A clean kitchen and dining hall are situated on the ground floor. The elders can have their breakfast, lunch, dinner, tea and snacks at this place. They can also have food and tea in their flat if they so wish. Those who cannot cook or are unable or unwilling to come to the hall are provided with the facility in their room itself. They can pay the monthly bill for their food or buy coupons. If the elders require food or tea beyond the stipulated timings, they can request for the service in advance.

There are tables and chairs set in the garden and the community hall for the elders to play indoor games. We saw some groups of elders enjoying this facility. There is also a small library that lends newspapers and books which is an excellent opportunity for those who love to read and increase their knowledge. Books are true friends and guides. The elderly need such true friends as they give them the inspiration to live life happily.

While discussing the concept of extended family it is but inevitable that the exemplary instance of Atahshri project established by Paranjpe schemes comes to mind. As I was acquainted with Mr.Shrikant Paranjpe I asked him what made him think of such a project. He replied with the joy and pride of a parent speaking about one's offspring. He was unstoppable in his enthusiasm.

He replied, Doctor, ours is a huge joint family. We belong to Parle. I have six uncles. My eldest uncle thought of a fantastic idea. He suggested that all the brothers stay in one complex but have separate households. One apartment could be reserved for common dining. Everyone must make it a point to have at least dinner together every day in the common dining and spend some time in each other's company. This arrangement would help to avoid differences and tensions arising from staying permanently together but would enable each one to share their joys and sorrows, give suggestions when required and help one another. Every one supported this idea. They brought the idea into practice but it continued only for a week. Mr. Shrikant Paranjpe was restless that this scheme had failed. Later he and his brother Shashank came to Pune for doing business and settled here. Their honesty and management skills won them success in their business. A large number of young Indians went abroad owing to their business or jobs and settled there. They were financially well off. They were emotionally close to their parents. Their parents who had spent a major part of their life in India would not feel comfortable to spend their post-retirement life abroad. These parents and children requested Mr. Paranjpe to find a solution for their problem.

The deep-rooted idea of an extended family resurfaced in Shrikant's mind, which was the genesis of the Athashri concept. A number of senior couples or even single senior citizens resided alone in bungalows in Pune. Their financial position was sound but for some reason they had to live alone and spend their time in loneliness. They faced several challenges such as maintaining a large house, scarcity of reliable support, irregular servants and the fear of being alone. There was no one to share one's feelings or turn to for help in times of difficulties. Life was a punishment for them. They wished to have a separate accommodation for themselves but also craved for company where they would feel safe, be able to share their joys and sorrows, chitchat leisurely, laugh and play and eat together.

Close relations are burdened with expectations, which further lead to disappointment and frustration and squabbles. The company of friends is a matter of choice. It is neither constant nor compulsory. There is no complete dependency and one is able to connive at shortcomings of the friends. Their expectations from each other are minimal. They are not constantly in each other's company and so are not likely to have conflicts. Such unencumbered friendship is always desirable otherwise familiarity breeds contempt. It provides the advantages of living close by, relationships free of expectations and conflicts. Athashri as a concept originated with the hope of realizing these dreams.

You must have heard the popular song, which assures us that

"God lends a hand to him who has no one

Just as by Him the burden of the suspended sky is borne!"

With a slight change we can now say

"Senior citizens without family support

Look up to Athashri as their resort!"

Mr. Paranjpe did not stop at just erecting the complex but continues to take feedback about the changing needs of the elders, discusses and continuously researches the issue and makes suitable changes. So while developing Phase- II he made arrangements for two bedroom flats also as well as guest rooms. This facility was meant for children, relatives and friends who would like to come and stay for a while. The guests are required to pay a minimum fee. They can avail of the dining facility also. We can avoid inconvenience by booking these rooms in advance.

Since Athashri is a residential complex of senior citizens a doctor visits each of them once a week to check up on their health. Health related data is carefully recorded and maintained in a file. An ambulance is kept ready in case any senior citizen is unwell and requires hospitalization. There is a tie up with certain hospitals to which these patients are sent. Since the health, related file is updated regularly and they have a tie up with the hospitals, time is not wasted in the preliminary formalities of admission. The family is informed about the patient because the responsibility till the patient recovers rests with the relatives.

Athashri members celebrate a number of festivals. The residents come together and organize entertainment programs, discussions, get together events annually. The Paranjpe family also participates in these programs, which also indicate the scope of the extended family. It will be appropriate to say,

"Senior citizens can depend upon the extended family of the Paranjpes for support."

There are six Athashri centers in Pune, Baroda and Bangalore.

Aastha Center

Athashri is a special residential scheme for the aged. Aastha is a care center established in 2007 meant for those senior citizens who are immobile, or those who have become handicapped due to illness and constantly require help. A medical practitioner is appointed here. The handicapped senior citizen is given a big room to stay in. There are toilet blocks, necessary furniture and an army of support staff constantly in service of the aged. The center doctor visits every week. Medicines prescribed by their own doctor are also given regularly to the patient. An ambulance is kept ready in case the patient needs to be shifted to a hospital and the relatives are promptly informed.

The security arrangement in these building complexes is very strong. Guests are not allowed into any apartment without the permission of the resident. Similarly, after you inform the security that the guest is leaving the security monitors that the guest has left the campus in reasonable time. An agency looks after the cleaning and mopping of floors, washing vessels and utensils in all the flats. In case their regular staff reports absent it is the responsibility of the agency to replace the person. This avoids a lot of inconvenience to the elders. Athashri takes care of all the repairs in the flats.

Since one owns the flat in Athashri the person does not feel that he or she is living in an old home. At the reception lobby as well as the flat doors name plates of the residents are displayed along with the floors. This develops a feeling of belongingness among the residents. A stipulated amount of money is charged for the services at the time of buying the house for a fixed period. After this period is over, maintenance charges have to be paid on a monthly basis or a few years, details about which can be discussed and finalized.

Since the resident is the owner of the flat, the resident can rent it to someone who needs it or even sell it off. One may take the help of the staff of Paranjpe Schemes or manage on one's own. A waiting list of sellers, those who wish to give the flat on rent as well as buyers is prepared.

With a view to constantly revise the concept of Athashri, currently a residential complex and a school have been erected near Forest Hill in Bhugaon. It is a nice effort to revive the elders' memories of their childhood in the company of the hullabaloo of the schoolchildren.

They say that a poet aspires to retain the child even in old age. The senior citizens would love to follow the poet's example and go down memory lane.

The members of Astha Center, Old age Homes, and Care Center are old and debilitated and are prone to suffer from depression. I wish to suggest that if in such centers informative VCDs about Stephen Hawkins are screened occasionally the aged will derive inspiration and believe that they can yet serve the society in their humble capacity. The life of someone who has suffered the worst of physical handicap for so long and who yet works as the director of Mathematics and Astronomy in Cambridge University can certainly motivate all the physically challenged elders and ward off their despair.

Home for the Aged
(Janseva Foundation)

The inevitability of establishing homes for the aged has come to stay in our society too. I felt that it was necessary to share the details of two such institutions. One is Athashri the extended family concept by Paranjpe schemes and the other is the old age home run by Dr. Vinod Shah of Janseva Foundation.

Serving the Old- The Need of the Times:

Inspired by the urge to accomplish social responsibility and discharge social obligation, led by the motto 'Service to Man is service to God', Dr. Shah established Janseva Foundation on 15 January 1988. The initial objectives of the Foundation were - spread health awareness by providing free or subsidized health care and medical aid to the poor and needy men and women in the society and by conducting medical examinations, eye care, health camps, medical exhibitions, lectures on topics related to health etc. Out of these activities emerged Janaseva Foundation's initiative of renovating the general hospital in Sonpur-Panshet area in association with Sahyadri Vikas Mandal.

We are all proud of our culture, which imbibes in us values that teach us to worship mother like god. Unfortunately, this belief seems to be fast disappearing. The joint family system that has been an essential aspect of the Indian society has now shattered completely. Many changes have occurred in the customs and traditions with the passing of time. As a part of this change, the single-family system has come into existence. Single families have started living in tall buildings but their minds are dwarfed. The society is greatly influenced by the concepts of privatization, liberalization, globalization and westernization. This is responsible for the declining morals and values of our society. In a way, the computers and television have reduced the physical distance between people but mentally and emotionally, an overwhelming distance has been created. It is possible to speak to someone who is actually on the moon (Mrs. Indira Gandhi spoke to astronaut Rakesh Sharma) but the sad part is the young do not speak to their parents who are right before their eyes and cannot establish communication with them. We hardly know who stays in the next-door flat or works in the neighboring office. Every one moves about with one's inflated ego and is unmindful of others. The feelings of love, respect, deference, affection seem to have vanished from people's relationships. Each one is conscious of one's own freedom and the accompanying rights but the young generation tries to avoid duties that come along with the rights.

In such circumstances the old feel isolated, feel sorry that they have become useless, loneliness, feel left out and insecure. The aged face lack of power, respect, financial independence, no planning of time and above all, they suffer from physical maladies due to old age. In such conditions, they expect help from their children but instead of being helpful to the parents the children are often thankless and irresponsible. A deep valley is created between the two which is generally termed as generation gap. Gradually a beautiful relationship starts wilting away.

The problems of the aged are rising in number as well as in magnitude. Hence, it is a big challenge before all of us to find solutions for the tribulations faced by the old.

We are slowly losing the rich cultural heritage of Indian culture that teaches us to worship our parents like God. The 'wada' housing system has given way to flats. The respect given to the eldest member of the family in the 'wada' system is now forgotten. Now we have family courts to settle disputes. In states like Hariyana and Maharashtra, the elders are entitled by law to receive maintenance from their children. It is a shame that we have to establish homes for the aged. The family system has broken down completely.

The aged face numerous problems such as familial, financial, health related issues, social, religious and many others. When I felicitated a seventy five year old person and presented him a shawl and a coconut, he commented that it would be better if they were respected in their own home rather than in such public programs.

As a person's age advances, the problems also increase. Old age is often considered as a predicament. I remember that a group of Rotarians once came to my consulting room to invite me to speak on the problems of the aged. At that time, an old man was sitting before me and he had put his head down on the table. When the group left, I tapped on his shoulder and asked him what had happened? Tears were flowing from his eyes. He said that since I was going to talk on the problems of the aged, he felt that ageing in itself was a big problem. He said, "God should have taken me away before this stage. I have come to you as a patient; I cannot hide the truth from you. I am sixty-three years old. My children have started troubling me ever since I retired. My wife died three years ago. Since I was not in a government job, I do not get any pension. My son has grabbed all my property along with my house and now it is in his name. He drinks every day, comes home, and beats me. My daughter in law also does not care for me. Therefore, I have come to you. Can you admit me into some home for the aged free of cost?" This conversation set me thinking that this issue regarding the aged is a very serious one.

It reminded of the lines from dramatist Kusumagraj's play 'Natsamrat'.

'Can someone give me a home?

(This master performer) This storm does not need a palace, nor a castle's set

No decorations, garlands or a bag full of money,

Just a small house to fold its wings and lie down,

And a rocking chair for the storm to recline.'

Janseva Foundation concentrates on four aspects viz., elder care, service to the destitute and handicapped, health care and social service. On the auspicious day of 15 January 1988 the Foundation began its social service at Sonapur, Ambi Ranawdi, Panshet which was inaugurated by respected Baba Maharaj Satarkar. But Baba Maharaj was not in favor of the idea of establishing a home for the aged. He was of the opinion that, "old age homes are against the Indian culture and the tradition of joint families. I feel that the day when old homes will be no more will be the most fortunate moment." He expressed his views on old homes very candidly. But taking into consideration the present social scenario and the decline of moral values, the old homes have become a necessity. Initially the Foundation brought together just a handful of old people and started its work.

The site of this work is situated 40 kms., away from Pune in the idyllic, pollution free natural surroundings of Ambi Ranawdi (Panshet). Trustee of the Foundation Shri Keshawrao Dhapre donated a plot of five acres in memory of his brother late Shri Govindrao Dhapre. With the help of a munificent donation received from Mr. Bharatbhai Sanghvi, a benevolent industrialist from Mumbai, Late Shrimati Kundangauri M. Sanghvi and Manharlal P. Sanghvi Complex came into existence. On the campus of this complex are situated the Foundation's projects such as home for the aged, rural hospital, mobile health care, eye hospital, center for the handicapped, nursing school and nurses' quarters, institute of education and cow sheds (goshala).

The old home building is spread over an area of 3760 square feet.

Initially, Janseva Foundation started a small old home in a rented space on the campus of the Sonapur General Hospital. They could take care of thirty to forty old people and charged nominal fees or none at all. Later when Jansewa Fondation was established, a building worth thirty lakh rupees was built after considering the requirements of the destitute and helpless inmates of the old home. Patron Mr. Nitinbhai Desai generously donated a large amount for the old home and so it has been named as Late Haribhai V. Desai Home for the Aged. Now the home can house up to one hundred senior citizens.

With the increase in the number of aged, another old home has been built. A sprawling building which can house sixty aged people, equipped with all the facilities required by them has been built for the cost of forty lakh rupees. This home for the aged was inaugurated on 19 February 1999, at the hands of the then Vice President of India Honorable Shri. Krushnakant. This home is named after the industrialist Shri Rasiklal

Manichand Dhariwal and his wife, Mrs. Shobha Dhariwal who donated generously for building this home.

From the donation received from the Khinwsara family Mrs. Icharbai Khinwsara residential complex has been erected.

Provision has been made to accommodate about fifty bedridden aged patients in need of medicine in the Paralytic Center for the aged.

Destitute old people are rehabilitated in the destitute rehabilitation center situated in Bhilarewadi, Katraj.

Haribhai V.Desai Home for the Aged phase II, is meant for those elders whose children have gone abroad and who are financially well off. This is a new facility ready with modern gadgets, equipments for exercise and other amenities. There are sixteen rooms for aged couples and provide facilities such as microwave oven, television, refrigerator, computer and internet, newspapers and books. The income received from this home is utilized to fund the expenses incurred on those poor seniors who are housed free of cost.

Senior citizens from not only economically weak families but also about one hundred and fifty elders from middle class and affluent families are also making use of this facility. The elders enjoy their stay here due to personal attention, round the clock availability of health care and a pleasant family like atmosphere. Among the inmates, there are twenty to thirty handicapped elders and five to ten old people who were previously treated in mental hospitals but were not accepted by their families even after they were cured. This must be the only institution that houses an old home and a hospital under one roof. Since the institution's nursing home is also close by the elders are benefitted by the services of the trained nurses. The Foundation has also developed facility for physiotherapy. The

Foundation has also set up a dairy project which supplies the aged with forty two litres of pure milk. On two and a half acres out of the five acre of the Ambi plot the Wanrai project has been developed by the Foundation's well wisher and advisor late Shri Mohan Dhariya. 'Wanrai', which is a forestation project, has cultivated and preserved one thousand different trees.

Senior citizens who do not live in the old homes but wish to spend time with other aged or wish to contribute to social work can avail of the day care facility jointly run by the Pune Municipality and Lions' Club of Pune Ganeshkhind, at the Baburao Genba Shewale hospital hall. For super senior citizens above the age of eighty the foundation runs six 'Shatayushi' Clubs in the city.

Most of the senior citizens suffer from cataract. The Foundation and Lions' Club of Aundh Pashan have launched an eye care hospital. Here one thousand free cataract surgeries are conducted annually. The Foundation's Late Comrade Govindrao Dhapre Hospital provides free medical care to senior citizens. Their projects, 'National Rural Health Project' and 'Mobile Healthcare Service' goes to different rural areas and provides services to the aged in their own villages.

With a view to raise awareness and encourage research along with rendering service to the aged, the Foundation has instituted a research center. This center has received recognition from Pune University for conducting research in gerontology, especially ageing and destitute care.

With financial support received from donors like Maharashtra Foundation-America, Share and Care-America, Shri Narendra Lakhani, Shri Anil Deshpande and other generous non resident Indians this research center has examined and treated 1238 senior citizens living in 38 villages. The investigations include pathological tests, x-ray, bone density test, ECG, cataract surgeries and medication. In case the patients require more attention, they are admitted to the hospitals for further treatment. The Foundation has published a book and a few research papers based on the research conducted in this center. Recently the Foundation successfully concluded a project on the health of the aged it had undertaken jointly with Duke University America and distributed water filters to the aged. The international company, Thyssen Krupp donated Sewage Treatment Plant to the foundation and a few medical equipments to the rural hospital under the CSR project. Sodhani Foundation has donated a bus.

Besides these activities, the Foundation celebrates Senior Citizens' day. Senior citizens who have made exceptional contribution in their field of work are felicitated on this day. Every four months a lecture by a renowned person is arranged under 'Meet the Stalwarts' program. Some of the distinguished personalities who have been interviewed are Padmavibhushan Dr. Mohan Dhariya, Padmavibhushan Dr. Raghunath Mashelkar, Padmavibhushan Dr. K. H. Sancheti, Padmabhushan Dr. S. B. Mujumdar, Padmashri Dr. Vijay Bhatkar and the veteran actor Dilip Prabhawalkar.

The Janseva Foundation has received Special Consultative Status from the United Nations Organization for all this work it has accomplished. The foundation has also received several awards for its service to society. Among the most remarkable is the 'Excellence in Social Work' award instituted by World Foundation on Reverence for All Life received at the hands of the then President of India Dr. Abdul Kalam. The Foundation was felicitated by the Pune Corporation, was given an Award for Excellence in Social Service by Chamber of Commerce and Agriculture and was awarded the highest distinction of 'Ambassador of Goodwill' by Lions' Club International. It also received the Vidhayak Karyakarta Award from Gandhi Memorial Committee, Aga Khan Palace,' Award of Excellence 'from Top Management Consortium as well as Maharashtra Government's 'Anandibai Puraskar' which is an award given to a social service institution for rendering best service to women. It also bagged the 'Servant of the Poor 'Award given by Confederation of NGOs (CNRI).Some other awards are the Pune Nawratri Mohotsav have given them 'Maharshi Puraskar' in 2013, Social service Award from Messrs. AP Traders and the Rashtriya Swayamsidhh Sanman Puraskar from JSPL Foundation (Jindal Steel and Power Ltd.).

Certainly after learning about the amount of service Dr. Vinod Shah has rendered to the cause of the old one feels that he deserves to be acknowledged and applauded on a national level.

Our wishes have come true because Janaseva Foundation has received Vayoshreshtha Samman Award under the Category of Best Institution for providing Services to Senior Citizens and Awareness Generation by the Ministry of Social Welfare and Empowerment, Govt. of India under Scheme of National Award for Senior Citizens for the year 2016.

Dr. Vinod Shah has been invited as an expert on Healthy Ageing to Regional Meeting on Healthy Ageing, Bangkok, Thailand from 26th – 28th October 2016 arranged by WHO Regional Office for South-East Asia.

Sincere congratulations to Dr. Vinod Shah. We all are extremely proud of his and Jansewa Foundation's achievement and wish them all the best!

For those Who Wish To Support Elders

Many a times we intend to do something for the society to mark birthdays and anniversaries. It is not possible to serve society directly every time. Hence we gain satisfaction by donating money for a certain cause. You may give such donations to Janaseva Foundation and feel assured that your gift will reach those individuals who really deserve help. You may also donate your free time to Janaseva Foundation and serve the needy elders.

Janaseva Foundation Old Age Home
Head Office

Janaseva Foundation, Indulal Complex, 1st floor, Above Rupee Bank, L.B.S. Road, Navi Peth, Pune – 411 030., Maharashtra, India.
Tel. +91 20 24538787/8,
Fax : +91 20 24537373.
Email : vinodshaha@hotmail.com

....

Ambi-Ranwadi, Tal. Velha, Dist. Pune
Contact - Dr. Vinod Shah
Phone - 24537373 / 9823011760, Email - vinodshaha@hotmail.com

During This Twilight

The Indian culture and its characteristic feature, the joint family system was venerated for a very long time. With the flow of time many good things have flown away, some have been completely shattered and some are on their way towards being destroyed. The force of change is so severe that we must try our best to preserve what we can from our traditions but at the same time accept changes wholeheartedly. One of the greatest advantages of the joint family system is that the family looks after the elders with care and respect in their old age. The younger generation could benefit from the elders' experience and their children could get love and affection as well as value education and guidance from the grandparents. The young couple could pursue their career without much bother. They did not have to worry about their home or children as the elders would take of them. The present fast and furiously competitive world has devalued the importance of all these facilities, love, and support. Everyone wishes to run faster and faster in the rat race and is just heading for the next station. By the time they realize what they have lost the younger generation will become old and will have reached the station of seniority.

While this prosperous tradition of the joint family was on the wane, a number of crèches and old homes started growing in number.Let us look at this transformation and facility from a positive point of view.

India is now largely urbanized. This creates a space crunch, financial shortage, a fast life style, the young couple's race for money, which hardly leaves any time for the young to speak at leisure with the old or spend quality time with them. Till both the elder husband and wife are together at least they can give each other company, inquire after each other's health and give emotional support. They spend their time in the company of their grand children. However, if the senior member is alone then she or he faces a tremendous amount of emotional starvation. The person feels very lonely. The elders make suggestions that may not be welcome and the young continue to jeer at the elders that are responsible for miscommunication or total lack of communication between the two generations. This situation further aggravates and they start insulting each other, show disrespect and even quarrel with each other. The lonely person keeps repeating these instances in her or his mind and becomes very sorrowful. The younger generation starts looking at the aged as an unnecessary burden and gradually the aged are compelled to take refuge in old homes or the young themselves send the old to old age homes. The aged leave their homes with a heavy heart and go to the old homes unwillingly. It is necessary that this sequence of events should now change. It is most desirable to be able to stay at home happily along with the family members by being able to adjust with the younger generation and giving up one's insistence on things. If this is not possible then instead of allowing bitterness to increase it is better to show maturity and move into an extended family in the form of home for the aged.

Instead of calling these institutions 'homes for the aged', it is better to call them 'support centers' or 'shelters' because that will create a positive attitude in the minds of the aged. Many founders of old homes have shown such sensitivity in naming their institutions. As these centers are situated in areas away from the busy rattle of the city they enjoy many advantages. They have ample space with a lot of greenery around. Fresh air, water, birds chirping at dawn and staff support is available. Unlike in the city there are no hassles so the seniors can spend time together in a leisurely fashion and share their joys and sorrows as if they belong to one big extended family. As they live in dormitories or on shared basis they do not feel lonely because they have their room partners for company. They can share their feelings among themselves. In case one does not get along with one person, there are others to choose.

They say prayers together, do bhajan and kirtan, attend lectures, play indoor games, listen to music, watch television or listen to the radio, read books and newspapers. They have their breakfast and food chitchatting with friends and enjoy life in the company of others. It is possible that when one is alone one may get bored of exercises but when in a group activities such as walking, swimming, yoga, exercises, pranayam and laughter yoga become stress busters. The mind becomes fresh and one feels enthusiastic. All this helps to increase the immunity of the body. The sorrows may not be completely forgotten but are considerably reduced. We all have often experienced that if we constantly focus on our physical pains they become unbearable. However, if we engage our mind in other happy thoughts the severity of the sorrow is blunted.

This experience is similar to the one when in the past small children used to go to their Guru's house, stay there and happily gain education. The number of elders coming to good old homes willingly is gradually rising. This must be considered as a positive change. The seniors must share their expertise, experience and knowledge gained through years of work with the other aged and give suggestions when required. The good old homes provide the aged facilities for medical examination and treatment. They also take the responsibility of admitting the aged to hospitals whenever required and promptly inform their relatives. Such homes have a tie up with hospitals and so the aged members are not required to pay deposit money for their treatment.

Some senior members have the habit of writing a diary or have the imaginative power for writing poems. They can make use of their time in a still more profitable manner. They can remain in touch with the world through laptop, smart phones, can upgrade their knowledge and get new information. They can share their knowledge with others, follow their hobbies and spend their time happily through these various measures. Each one should engross oneself in one's own field of interest. If one is not interested in hobbies, one can do a bit of gardening and spend time fruitfully.

Since in these homes all the members are aged, they are contemporaries, they can share similar sorrows as well as thoughts, and so can spend time together, meaningfully. This helps to forget stress and tension. The feeling, that there is someone around to take care is very reassuring. Life gains a new meaning because of this. So instead of Ageing it becomes age conservation.

If we do not get along well with the new generation, if we feel that the other's presence in the house is troublesome, should we yet continue to sing in praise of the advantages of the joint family under the pressure of what people might say? Instead of continuing to suffer in dissatisfaction and wait miserably for the end to come, it is always advisable to take the help of some good old age home. According to the Vedic tradition, life is divided into brahmacharyashram, gruhasthashram, vanprasthashram and sanyasaashram. This arrangement must have been made after taking into consideration the various problems man faces in life and the differences in thoughts and behavior between two generations.

An acquaintance asked a widow whose two sons lived abroad, "how do you stay alone? Don't you feel afraid? Aren't you bored?" Her answer is an example of how one can be very positive and face all the circumstances joyfully. She replied," I am not alone in the house. We are three of us, the first is I, the second is the telephone and the third is the television.

We should observe that the woman did not blame either god or fate or her children for her sorrow but brought in positive changes in her thoughts and adopted a suitable life style which made her feel contented.

In short, we can say that during this twilight we can avoid the feeling of loneliness, hopelessness if we accept a positive point of view. An optimistic attitude keeps the mind calm and makes it possible to live through the twilight of life under a peaceful starry sky.

There is bound to be a gap in the thoughts of two generations. Both the generations should refrain from insisting that only one of them is right. It is not proper to expect the new generation to change according the ideas of the old. It is not proper to find faults with the younger generation. It is useless to rue over what has changed. We are ready to accept the fruits of development like vehicles, television, phone, long distance tours. We have to bear the disadvantages also such as pollution and radiation. If we wish to enjoy the advantages, we should be ready to suffer the disadvantages too.

Every one young and old must accept what is inevitable and give up all that can be avoided. It is of no use to detest one or the other generation.

The Swan Song of Life

For thousands of years people believed that if we won God's grace we would be showered with boons while God's wrath would bring doom and untold miseries. This fear of God made people behave ethically. They also thought that even if the body was perishable the soul was immortal. The soul enters a new body after the death of the previous one. If we wish to be reborn as humans, we are required to accumulate a large amount of good deeds in the earlier birth. So the human beings strictly followed a code of conduct given in the form of religion. Even now, the theists staunchly support the ideas of god –religion or good and bad deeds.

As science developed and the cause effect relationship between natural events was revealed, man became more knowledgeable and slowly the philosophy of atheism started spreading among people. The number of agnostics or non-believers is more in the developed or advanced countries while there are many believers in the under developed countries. Some prefer to sit on the fence and keep dangling between belief and non-belief. They are convinced that there is no such entity as god but just in case there exists one why should one unnecessarily speak against her or him and invite the deity's fury. They safely decide their faith or otherwise according to the situation. Human beings love permanence. It is quite natural to feel uncomfortable and insecure while accepting change and hence accepting change takes a lot of time.

Bound by the principles of religion man accepts to abide by some good principles such as truth, non-violence, avoids greed, does charity and follows ethical values. This is one of the plus points of traditional spiritualism. The person is afraid of death and so does good deeds with the hope that she or he will be reborn in a better form. Truly speaking, death is the end of our existence. In order to inspire man to commit good deeds and help reduce the dreadfulness of death, concepts such as the soul and rebirth are very useful. If man is convinced of the inevitability of death and that she or he should do all the good deeds possible in this birth, only because there is no rebirth the person might pursue an ideal path of life. On the other hand, those ill-natured persons who follow the wrong path will have no threat of the consequences of their sins in the after birth and will recklessly continue on the vicious path of life. In fact even those people who believe in god and virtues are seen to be practicing evil ways. They perform the rituals of worship of their religion; chant the name of their God and attack shrines of other religions. Trustees of the temples do not hesitate to swindle money from those very temples; their hands do not tremble while robbing ornaments offered to the deity. They are not afraid of anything at all. In case there is an iota of fear, avarice takes the better of trepidation. In short, it is evident that greed has won over the fear of god and following religious principles.

All the religions of the world, philosophies and spirituality are wound round the concepts of death, hell, soul and rebirth. Even if it is difficult for the intelligent human being, it is not impossible for him to disentangle himself from these thoughts with the help of rationalism and knowledge. Science has defined death. As long as the inert body receives energy from food and oxygen, it is alive. Science has proved that death is not caused because the soul leaves the body but when this power supply is blocked for some reason it leads to death.

Spiritualists call the transfer of the soul from one to another body as reincarnation. Every DNA continues through reproduction, which in other words could be called its rebirth. Science proves that genealogy is preserved in this manner.

Naive people believe the stories about rebirth, which the newspapers or cinemas project. There are people who claim to have experienced the things they see now for the first time in their previous births. If we search for and examine such reports of the past hundred years carefully preserved in some countries, which create an illusion of rebirth there is no evidence to prove such claims. Nevertheless, these negations are not made public. Researchers of the human brain have studied such occurrences that they term as 'déjà vu'. The scientific reason behind such experiences is the temporary miscommunication between the limbic system and the cortex. This creates an illusion of having experienced the present event or scene even in the past.

Religious scriptures and spiritualists speak of the body as perishable but the soul is immortal. They describe the soul as that which is 'unscathed by any weapon' 'cannot be burned by any fire' and 'cannot be decimated'. If the energy in the body is called soul, even energy is imperishable. Science has undoubtedly proved that "both the body and the soul both are everlasting. The store of energy and matter in the universe is eternal though it may constantly undergo transformation. They can neither be created nor destroyed."

In short, both the body and the soul are perpetual. The finite truth is that their forms may keep on changing. Both the rationalists and spiritualists insist that we must have a positive attitude towards life.

A simple, spiritualist, common person might describe the glass of water as half filled or half empty. However, an advocate of science will describe it as completely filled, half with water and the other half with air.

Spiritualism believes that the beginning or end of life is not in our hands. Science has been able to refute this claim also. It is possible to preserve sperms and eggs for years together with the help of advanced techniques and man can decide when to fertilize them and give birth to a new life. It is also possible with the help of advancement in science and technology to postpone death from certain diseases or mishaps, which in the past would have proved fatal. In the past if there was, bleeding in the brain due to an accident, or the person suffered a severe heart attack that stopped the entire heart function it meant certain death. The progress in the field of medicine can now save the life of such patients.

Whatever the age of the person is, the person should never end the struggle of life. We must try to live the best quality, healthy life. However, if the person is suffering from painful diseases such as cancer or if life has become too miserable to tolerate then the person should try with all his might and his body to be of help to others. One must develop the willingness and the ability to donate.

Many strong minded people who suffer from excruciating pain helplessly await death or beg to be given death. Allowing them to die before death comes naturally to them is called 'euthanasia'. This issue of mercy killing was debated heatedly on many international forums. Many countries have legalized euthanasia. If a committee of medical experts, legal experts and social workers approve of mercy killing it is like a boon for the suffering person. If such a person expresses his wish for organ donation before or after death, his wish should be respected. This is possible for all except those patients suffering from HIV, cancer or other contagious diseases. If within six hours, the cornea removed from these patients is transplanted to those suffering from corneal opacity it is possible to help minimum two patients and maximum six to regain their eyesight and come out of the dark pit of blindness. Organ donation is great charity. Along with the eyes if those organs that are healthy are removed a few hours before death or immediately after death and are transplanted into the needy patients within two hours after removal they will be able to lead a better life. They may also save someone's life. Organs such as the heart, heart valves, blood vessels, kidney, liver, bones, bone marrow, skin, pancreas all can be useful.

If the body is donated after a long time after death then it can be used in medical colleges for the students to learn anatomy of the human body. But this does not serve any noble purpose, as it does not directly help to increase or improve someone's life. The life span of the past generations which followed spirituality was very short. It is self evident that the development made by science has increased human longevity. Even if we have been successful in postponing death we cannot avoid it completely. Death is inevitable. Hence, man's search for immortality goes on.

Logic of the seers stops at the idea of death.

We must not cling to old ideas and stay in the darkness of ignorance.

Let us pray:

'May the darkness of vice set and see the sun of one's own religion rising

May each living being be granted his heart's longing! '

Saying this, let us hope to destroy ignorance and age-old ideas with the help of the light of scientific knowledge.

Annexure

Heart, Brain, Cancer & Kidney Charitable Trusts

Rajiv Gandhi Jeevandayee Arogya Yojana Society ESIS Hospital Compund, Ganpat Jadhav Marg, Worli Naka Worli Mumbai – 400018	**Chief Minster Relief fund** Secretary to the Hon Chief Minister, Mantralaya, Mumbai - 400032
SHRI SAIBABA SANSTHAN TRUST, Shirdi Shirdi Dist Ahemdnagar	Shree Siddhivinayak Ganapati Temple Trust Shree Siddhivinayak Ganapati Temple Trust, Prabhadevi, Mumbai
Distict Health Officer Distict Hospital	**Shivamrut Sarva vanchit vikas sanstha** Vijaynagar, Akluj, Taluka Malshiras, Dist Solopur.
Oswal Bandhu Samaj 321/A, Vardhaman, Mahatma Phule Peth, Opp. Hotel Seven Love's, Mahatma Phule Peth, Jawaharlal Nehru Rd, Agarwal Colony, Sadar Bazaar, Pune, Maharashtra 411042	**Late. Chandukaka Saraf Charitable Trust** Gandhi Chowk, Baramati

Rohan Builders "The Reverie, First Floor, 805, Bhandarkar Institute Road, Pune: 411 004, Maharashtra, INDIA."	**Shri Shanaishwar Devasthan** Shanishingnapur, Post: Sonai,Taluka: Nevasa,Dist.: Ahamednagar, Pin. 414 105, Maharashtra, India.
Shriman R.R Rathi Trust Ashirwad Chandak Garden, Budhwar Peth Soloapur	**Shri Mahalaximi Charitable trust** Bhulabhai Desai road Mumbai 4000026
Shivkalyan Vikas Sanstha 72, Kondhwa Khurd Pune 411048	**Diwaliben Meheta Trust** Khatu Mansion,Omar Park, 95 Bhulabhai Desai Road, Mumbai-36
IndoGerman Social Service Society 38 Lodhi Road, Institute Area New Delhi 110003	**Jivdani Devi Mandir Trust** Virar East,Taluka Vasai, Dit Thane
N.R Baldota Foundation N.R. Baldota Foundation near Hotel Shangrila chiplun road pune - 411001.	**Shri Gajanan Maharaj Sansthan, Shegaon** Tq. Shegaon - 444203 Dist- Buldana(M.S.)
Dagadusheth Halwai Ganapati Temple 250, Budhwar Peth, Ganpati Bhavan, Shivaji Road, Pune, Maharashtra 411002	**M/S. V.D Gosavi Co.** M/s V.D Gosavi company 244 Narayan Peth Laxmi Road, Pune
Shri Mahabaleshwar Mandir Trust Mahabaleshwar Tal Vai Dist Satar	**Goodluck Nerolac Paints Charitable Trust** Ganpatrao Kadam Marg Lower Parel Mumbai

N.M Wadia Charitable Trust 123,M.G Road Mumbai-1	**SHAPOORJI PALLON-JI CHARITY TRUST** New India Centre, 11th floor, Kuperaj, Maadaam Yuri Road, Mumbai
Venkatesh Hatcheries Sinhgad Rasta Vitthal Wadi Pune	**Chairman, Chaitanya Posna Trust** Gondawale Bk, Taluka Mann, Dist Satara
Mahaveer Heart Foundation Avanti Apartment, Flank Road, Sion, Mumbai 400022, Opposite Gandhi Market, Near Sanmukhanand Hall	**Bai Freni & Seth Fali Meherji Variava Charitable Trust** c/o Blaze Tours & Travels Pvt. Ltd.Lalji Naranji Memorial Bldg, 3rd floor, Opp. Churchgate Station, Mumbai - 400 020
Wattmul Foundation dollar first floor magas road patkar marg Mumbai-36	**Shri Swami Samarth** Shivsena Bhavanjal,Dadar Mumbai
Rameshwardasji Birla Smarak Kosh Medical Research center,Bombay Hospital Mumbai-20	**Allana Foundation** Allana House Alana Road Kulaba Mumbai-1

Essential Certificates and Documents

The Government of Maharashtra, under the Jeevandayi Aarogya scheme , gives financial support to poor patients living under the poverty line for carrying out surgeries related to the heart , brain, cancer and kidney. In order to avail of this facility the following documents are essential:

1. A request letter from the patient or the patient's parents

2. Budget of the proposed surgery

3. Medical Certificate

4. Income Certificate from Tehsildar (Mamledar Office)

5. After getting income certificate from the Tehsildar an affidavit on a Rs.100 stamp, stating the family income (From Mamledar or Notary)

6. If the patient is a resident of a village then a domicile certificate from Gramsevak or Sarpanch is required. If the patient lives in a city the domicile certificate should be sought from the Municipality. Those below poverty line should bring a certificate from the Tehsildar certifying that the person has been a resident of Maharashtra for fifteen or more years.

7. Xerox copies of the first and last pages of the ration card.

8. Certificate of the Block Development Officer (Panchayat Samiti Office), and registration number in the records of the under poverty line survey completed in 2002 with BDO's signature and round seal. (Take

below poverty line certificate from Gram Sewak and submit to the BDO)

9. Four Passport size photographs of the patient

10. Three original copies of recommendation from MLA (Amdar) (These are required to be attached to the application made to Hon. Chief Minister, Shirdi Saibaba Trust,and Siddhivinayak Trust)

11. Certificate from MP (Khasdar) to be attached with application made to the Prime Minister's relief Fund. (Do not make Xerox copies of certificates received from MLA or MP)

- Out of the charity institutions whose addresses are mentioned overleaf, twenty institutions require the documents and Xerox copies of certificates referred above. You will have to get twenty copies of the documents number one to eight, attested by a special officer or head of an educational institution and submit them.

- Those under the poverty line need not submit certificate no. eight.

- It will take a month or two to receive financial help from charity institutions and hence it is necessary that the papers be submitted as soon as possible.

- Financial help is given only if the applications are submitted prior to the surgery.

- The patient or the patient's family member submits the application to the charitable trust or foundation. The trust scrutinizes the application according to the terms and conditions of the trust and the amount is sanctioned according to the availability of funds. This is intimated to the patient on her/his residential address.

- It is necessary to send the patient's photograph along with the application made to the Prime Minister's National Relief Fund.

- While applying to the Shri Shirdi Sai Baba institution it is necessary to submit income affidavit in the original. Patients below poverty line should submit two copies of the income affidavit.

- The forms required for seeking aid from Shirdi Sansthan, Sidddhivinayal Nyas, Oswal Brothers and Chaitanyaupasana are available at Giriraj Hospital.

- Financial aid received for angioplasty, open-heart surgery, dialysis, scan, ECG, is around thirty to forty percent of the expenses incurred in Pune or Mumbai.

For Family Members of Government and Semi-Government Employees

The Government and Semi-Government employees can receive financial support for their family members in case of heart, kidney and brain surgeries. For receiving an advance of one and a half lakh rupees, they should attach the following documents along with their application.

1   Application of the employee for advance

2   Hospital quotation

3   Medical certificate

4   Family certificate (from Talathi)

5   Xerox copy of ration card

6   Undertaking of the employee regarding advance

7   Copy of the letter by Government recognising Giriraj Hospital

8   Children certificate (Employee)

9   Certificate stating that the surgical facility is not available in the nearby government hospital

10 Certificate of Permanent status in the job

11 Certificate that the school or college is government aided

12 Do not send the surgery and treatment bills from government recognized hospitals to the Civil Hospital for reimbursement. The angioplasty bills can be reimbursed.

13 For State Transport employees it is mandatory to register the name of the patient with the Medical Officer, Baramati Depot, before she/he undergoes surgery.

Sample of Recommendation from (MP, MLA)

This is to certify that Shri/Shrimati ------------------------- resident of ------------ (taluka) -------------- (district) is known to me. He/She is to undergo -------------------surgery in -------------------------hospital. The estimated expenses for the surgery is expected to be -------------------------.

Shri/Shrimati ------------------------'s economic condition is poor. She/He will not be able to bear the expenses and hence She/He requires financial aid.

(Note: Three letters from MLA /MP)

Signature and Stamp

SAHYOG TRUST

Education for all. Life for all

Public Trust Act. No. F 1688 Yavatmal / 87,

Society Registration Act No. Maharashtra / 1625/87

Head Office: No. 1, Prathamesh CHS, Prabhat Road Lane No. 5, Pune - 411004.

website: www.sahyogtrust.in, Phone. No. 020-25459777, Fax.25457222

Greetings to every one !

Since we are convinced about the concept of 'euthanasia' a few of us in Pune are researching it and working on it. The members who are participating in this programme under the aegis of Sahyog Trust are Dr. Shirish and Aarti Prayag (Medicine), Aseem and Rama Sarode (Law), Mangala Athlekar, Dr. Rohini Patwardhan (Elder Care), Shubhada Joshi, Vidya Bal and Ravindra Gore.

We have selected the topic of 'living will' in order to create general awareness about this extensive position on 'euthanasia'. We have attached a sample of the format of living will along with this article. If you concur with our thoughts and feel that the format is adequate, kindly fill up the form, (retain a copy with you) and send it to us on the above-mentioned address. You may even simply intimate us about your will. You may also suggest changes in the format if required. We will happily welcome those suggestions.

It is necessary to remember one very important point regarding the living will. It is not enough that you write it and just keep it. You should discuss the details regarding the choices to be made about selecting medical treatment with those who will be involved in making those decisions such as husband/wife, son/daughter, and daughter in law/son in

163

law and find out what their opinion on the topic of ' mercy killing' is. In the case where they differ in their views, we must make sincere efforts to transform their views. This is important because these are going to be the people who will be carrying out your wishes when you die. In case they are not of the same mind as you, what will happen is that when after dying, since you cannot communicate, these people will set aside the living will you have scripted and follow their own wishes. Hence, it is necessary to make a living will, share the contents of the will with the family members and take their consent.

It is necessary that the family doctor should sign on the living will. Besides this, you must share your will with young, healthy, educated neighbours, colleagues in the work place and ask them to sign as witnesses. Even your lawyer's signature should be taken.

Based on the forms that you will fill, we are trying to submit a PIL, public interest litigation, in order to receive legal sanction to euthanasia. We wish to append your living will along with the PIL. We shall attach your form only if you do not object to its use. Therefore, if you are agreeable to this arrangement, only then kindly send the form duly filled to our office.

It is not that once you prepare a living will, it cannot be revised. You can make changes periodically if required.

We look forward to receive a positive response from you.

Yours truly

Dr. Rohini Patwardhan - 9421081181
Adv. Rama Sarode   - 9822532137
Ravindra Gore   - 9011061961
Shubhada Joshi   - 9822034597

LIVING WILL

TO MY FAMILY, DOCTOR, AND ALL THOSE CONCERNED WITH MY HEALTH CARE:

1. I, ... aged ...., residing at ....direct you to follow my wishes for care if I am in a terminal condition, my death is imminent and I am unable to communicate my decisions about my medical care.

2. I am well verse with the concept of Right to Life enshrined the Indian Constitution and I am also aware about fundamental right of Freedom of Expression. I support the idea of living with human dignity and dying with same esteem.

3. With respect to any life-sustaining treatment, I direct the following:

   A. If my death is imminent or I am permanently unconscious, I choose not to prolong my life. I do not wish to inject myself from various places in my body and live in a disgusting situation.

   B. If life sustaining treatment has been started I request you to stop it especially if the life sustaining treatment is not going to help me live a dignified life but is merely going to prolong my life meaninglessly.

   C. If I am terminally ill, death is imminent or I am permanently unconscious or the chances of me coming to consciousness are very bleak then I request you not to provide me artificial nutrition and hydration. I wish to reiterate that I wish to reject giving me any life support in the above mentioned situations.

D. I know that on the basis of my wishes mentioned herein doctors suggestions can be sought for. I also know that any committee of medical practitioners can be also consulted. But as the Law is very clear on this issue which says that when any person stops talking his or her 'Will' starts speaking. Hence it is my request to all persons who love me to respect my living will.

4. This living will is made to let people know who love me and care for me that I do not want to be kept alive in a state where I am not able to live a normal life and there is no guarantee that I will be in a conscious state to take my decisions. Hence if there is any other consideration that has to be done and is missing in this will I request you to take a wise decision and respect my wish of not keeping me alive just for the sake of it.

I am making this Living Will of my own conscious decision and without anyone's pressure.

IN WITNESS WHEREOF, I the said Mr. Dilip Dharmadhikari do hereby set and subscribe my hand to this my last Living Will at Pune in the presence of witnesses on this day of......

Signed by the above named

As his last Living Will in
The presence of us both being present
At the same time who in his presence
And in the presence of each other
Have hereunto set and subscribed our
Names as witnesses

1)

2)

For those Who Wish To Support Elders

Many a times we intend to do something for the society to mark birthdays and anniversaries. It is not possible to serve society directly every time. Hence we gain satisfaction by donating money for a certain cause. You may give such donations to HelpAge India and feel assured that your gift will reach those individuals who really deserve help. You may also donate your free time to HelpAge India and serve the needy elders. HelpAge India requires M.B.B.S. doctors and pharmacists as well as social workers and drivers to keep its 120 mobile medical centres functional.

HelpAge India

9/67, Phule Nagar, Behind Alandi Road R.T.O. Ground
Near Bodhichitta Vihar, Pune - 411006, Maharashtra
Contact - Rajeev Kulkarni
Phone - 020 20265513 / 09422020699 / www.helpageindia.org.

HelpAge India Office Addresses
as on 01st April 2016

• *Delhi (Head Office)*	HelpAge India C-14, Qutab Institutional Area New Delhi - 110016 Toll Free Elder Help Line: 1800-180-1253 –
• *Jammu*	Contact Person: Ms. Sunita Santoshi Manager Address: House No. 27, Gandhi chowk Behind Shiv Mandir Subhash Nagar Jammu - 180005 Jammu & Kashmir Ph.: 0191-2560141 Mobile: 09419140619 / 09419144551

• *Srinagar*	Contact Person: Mr. Syed Ajaz Social Protection Officer Address: Alamgari Bazar Auqaf Market OPP. Govt. Dispensary Srinagar - 190001 Jammu & Kashmir Ph.: 0979633973
• *Shimla*	Contact Person: Dr. Rajesh Kumar State Head – Himachal Pradesh Address: Lady Harding Cottage (No.3) Near H.P. High Court Bambloe, Shimla - 171001 Himachal Pradesh Ph.: +91-0177-2811254 Mobile: 09418977457 / 09816033457 –
• *Chandigarh (Panjab)*	Contact Person: Mr. Bhavneshwar Sharma State Head – Punjab, Chandigarh, Haryana & J&K Address: House No. 5745 (Ground Floor) Sector 38– West Chandigarh – 160038Punjab Ph.: 0172-6542268 / 2620869 Mobile: 09417456864 Fax: 0172-2716112
• *Dehradun (Uttarakhand)*	Contact Person: Mr. Chaitanya Upadhyay Acting State Head – Uttarakhand Address: 53-B, 137 Rajpur Road Dehradun - 248001 Uttarakhand Ph.: 0135-2655535/2711927 Mobile: 8171927453
• *Jaipur (Rajasthan)*	Contact Person: Mr. Nilesh Kumar Girishbhai Nalvya State Head – Rajasthan Address: Plot No 3, Shiv Marg behind Raj Bhawan Civil Lines Jaipur – 302006 Rajasthan Ph.: 0141-2220241 Mobile: 09587237317
• *Lucknow*	Contact Person: Mr. A. K. Singh State Head – Uttar Pradesh Address: 3/129, Vikas Nagar Lucknow – 226022Uttar Pradesh Ph.: 0522-2738048/ 2738054 Mobile: 09415010645
• *Patana (Bihar)*	Contact Person: Mr. Girish Chandra Mishra State Head – Bihar Address: House No. 134 Patliputra Colony Patna - 800013Bihar Ph.: 0612-2273271
• *Guwahati*	Contact Person: Mr. Nilondra Tanya Deputy Director – Programs Address: 17, Rukminigaon, Bylane No.6 (1st floor) Guwahati – 781022 Assam Ph.: +91 361 222 8330 Mobile: +91 8011527423
• *Varanasi*	Contact Person: Ms. Aditi Singh Address: HelpAge India D 63/A, Govindpur SK Shivpurwa, Near Grand Palace Marriage Hall Varanasi - 221010 Uttar Pradesh

• *Ahmedabad*	Contact Person: Mr. Anil Massey State Head - Gujarat Address: 407, 4th Floor Mistry Chambers Vidya Gauri Nilkanth Marg near CAMA Hotel, Khanpur Ahmedabad - 380001 Gujarat Ph.: 079-25601441
• *Bhopal*	Contact Person: Ms. Sanskriti Khare State Head – Madhya Pradesh Address: A-98, Shanti Kunj Sector-A Shahpura, Mansarover Colony Bhopal - 462016,
• *Kolkata*	Contact Person: Ms. Sharmila Majumdar Territory Head - West Bengal & North East Address: Flat No 406, 162- B 4th Floor, A.J.C. Bose Road Kolkata - 700014 West Bengal Ph.: 033-32904121/ 22492526
• *Indore*	Address: HelpAge India 169, A Viswash Nagar Gram - Banjari Bhatkhedi Opposite Hotel Manal Tehsil- Mhow Indore - 453441 Madhya Pradesh
• *Chhattisgarh*	Contact Person: Mr. Subhankar Biswas State Head – Chhattisgarh Address: C/o: Dr. B. C. Gupta, Shantikunj, Budhapara, Raipur - 492001 Chhattisgarh Ph.: 0771 2534498/4014401 Mob: 9433039332, 9893295602
• *Nagpur*	Contact Person: Mr. S. V. Thakur Senior Manager – Resource Mobilization Address: A–Wing, Flat–8 Parishram Co–Op Housing Society Narendra Nagar, Opp. Hanuman Mandir Nagpur - 440015 Maharashtra Ph.: 0712-2759639 Mobile: 09822471313
• *Mumbai*	Contact Person: Mr. Prakash N. Borgaonkar Territory Head – Maharashtra, Goa & Gujrat Address: No. 34 – A/44, Guruchhaya Manish Nagar, P. O. Azad Nagar Andheri (W) Mumbai – 400053 Maharashtra Ph.: 022-26370754 / 40 Mobile: 09821224513
• *Pune*	Contact Person: Mr. Rajeev S. Kulkarni Manager – Resource Mobilization Address: 9/67, Phule Nagar Behind Alandi Road R.T.O. Ground Near Bodhichitta Vihar, Pune - 411006 Maharashtra Ph.: 020-20265513
• *Bhubaneswar*	Contact Person: Ms. Bharati Chakra State Head - Odisha Address: Plot No: N2 -157 IRC Village, Nayapalli Bhubaneswar - 751015 Odisha Ph.: 0674-2559644 Mobile: 09437104104

• Visakhapatnam	Contact Person: Mr. Mrinal Srikanth Lankapalli Manager - AP Address: H. No. 1-70-10, Plot No. 91/3 Sector – III, M.V.P. Colony Visakhapatnam – 530017 Andhra Pradesh Ph.: 0891-2721253 Mob: 09966001594
• Hyderabad	Contact Person: Mr. Mohd. Raza Mohammed Acting State Head Address: 2-2-3/A/A5, Prema Sai Bhuvanam Apartments beside ATI Shivam Road, DD Colony Hyderabad – 500007 Telangana Ph.: 040-27427066 / 27428472 Mobile: 09440474984
• Goa	Contact Person: Mr. D. M. Pawaskar Manager – Resource Mobilisation Address: House No 1342, Plot No. 21 Near Hanuman Temple, Next to Central Bank Housing Board Colony Porvorim, Bardez, Goa – 403521 Ph.: 0832-2412611 Mobile: 09822162642
• Cuddalore (Tamilnadu)	Contact Person: Mr. Venugopal Ramalingam Head –Project Management Officer Address: Tamaraikulam Elders Village Periyakankanankuppam (Opp. RK ITI) Subauppalavadi Post Cuddalore - 607002 Tamil Nadu Ph.: 04142-212352/53/54 Mobile: 09840696445
• Chennai	Contact Person: Mr. V Siva Kumar Joint Director - Resource Mobilization, Tamil Nadu Address: 3–C, Thiagaraja Complex 853, Poonamallee High Road Kilpauk, Chennai - 600010 Tamil Nadu Ph.: 044-25322149 Mobile:+91-9443831333, +918220044050 Tele Fax: 044-26480874
• Bangalore	Contact Person: Ms. Rekha Murthy State Head - Karnataka Address: 113, Royal Corner No 1 & 2 Lal Bagh Road Bangalore – 560 027 Karnataka Ph.: 080-22213107/22124594
• Puducherry	Contact Person: Mr. C. Manikandan Agecare Coordinator Address: Agecare Puducherry Sr. Citizens' Fitness and Wellness Centre No. 13 Aurobindo Street Puducherry - 605001 Ph.: 0413-2222095 Mobile: 09894952639
• Kochi (Kerala)	Contact Person: Mr. Biju Mathew State Head – Kerala Address: 39/5370, 4th Cross Road Panampilly Nagar Ernakulam (Kochi) Kerala - 682036 Ph.: 0484-2310836/4036118 Mobile: 09447209678

Old Age India Office Addresses

as on 01st April 2016

MAHARASHTRA	
Babusaheb Firodia Vridhashram Nagar, Aurangabad Road, Near Vasant Tekadi. Mr. Rusi - 0241-2225971	**Kasturba Sarvodaya Manadal** Madhan P O Chandur Bazar, 444 704. Secretary - 0722-2243236
Madhuban Vrudhashram Kondheshwar Road, Badnera, 444 701. **Mr. narayan Mishra** **0721-22679035**	**Matoshree Old Age Home (1995)** Kathora Naka, Vidharbha Mahavidyala, Amravti-444604, Maharashtra **Mr. S. G. Raut - 9764714880**
Mukti Sopan Nyas 178, Samarth Nagar, Aurangabad- 431001 **Mrs. Karandikar / Mr. B.B. Belsare.** **0240-2320045/ 9325988417**	**Matoshri Vruddhasharam** Paithan Road, Aurangabad, Maharashtra **Mr. Pagore - 240-2379111 /** **09850607818**
Aastha Foundation Gut No. 26 (PT), At Jadgaon,, Tongaon, Aurangabad, Maharashtra 431005 090112 84888 **Mr. Jayant Sangwikar - 9325202897**	**Manavlok - Marathawada** **Navnirman Lokayat** Dhadpad Office, Po. Box No.23, Ring Road, Ambajogai, 431 517. **Dr. D. S. Lohiya** **02446-247116, 247217**
Maharogi Seva Samiti, Warora Home for the Leprosy, A/P Anandwan, Tal. Warora, 492 914. **Mr. Kaustubh Vikas Amte** **07176-2282034, 2282425, 9922440006**	**Navajivan Vidya Vikas Mandal** A/Po. Naigaon, **Mr. Shashikant Tukaram Bhadane** **02562-223128**
Navajivan Vidya Vikas Mandal 11, Om Building, Borse Nagar, Gondur Road. **Mr. Shashikant Tukaram Bhadane** **- 9423193867**	**Norgyeling Tibetan Old Age Home** Representative Off., Norgyeling Tibetan Settlement, Po. Pratapgarh, 441 702. **Ven Thupten - 07196-226108**
Alice Home Kolhapur Diocesan Council C/O Bishop's Office, E.P. School Compund, 416 003 **Bishop of Kolhapur - 0231-2654832**	**Chakshus Home** Address: 2707 B ward Mandlik Galli, Mangalwar Peth,Kolhapur - 416012.

Shrivimleshwar Registerd Charity Institute, Siddhai Apartment, 96-2 A Ward, Near Vikas Highschool, Dudhali, Kolhapur - 416003. 0231 - 2547090.	**Shree Foundation,** Address: Shanti Sadan, Shivajinagar Peth, Vadgaon, Kolhapur - 416112. **Phone : 0230 - 2471914.**
Shri Datta Sevabhavi Sanstha, A/P - Narsobawadi, Tal- Shirol, Narsobawadi, Kolhapur - 416104 **Mobile : +(91) - 9623955429.**	**Sanskar Wachanalaya Bhadole** At Post - Bhadole, Hatkanangle, Kolhapur - 416109. **Phone : 0230 - 2409085.**
Shri Venkatashwara Gramin Vikas Sanstha Madilage A/P- Madilage, Taluka - Bhudargad, Gargoti, Kolhapur - 416209 **Phone : 02324 - 235834.**	**Sanjeevani Social Foundation** At Post - Sangrul, Tal - Karveer, Kolhapur - 416526. **Mobile : +(91) - 9423044231.**
Republican Social Foundation, House No. 905/2 A/1, Devakar Panand, A Ward, Kolhapur - 416012 **Phone : 0231 - 2240257.**	**Rashtraseva Samajik Vikas Sanstha,** At Post - Talsande, Hatkanangle, Kolhapur - 416109. **Phone : 0230 - 2479106.**
Pandurang Rukmini Vikas Seva Sanstha Mahagond, At - Mahagond, Taluka- Ajara, Kolhapur - 416220. **Phone : 02323 - 221510.**	**Nesari Vachan Mandir,** Smarak Road, At - Nesari Taluka - Gadhinglaj, Nesari, Kolhapur - 416504. **Phone: 02327 - 271925.**
Navasandesh Vachanalay Va Sanskrutik Sanstha Wadakshivale - **+(91) - 9405854548.**	**M.N Roy Institute,** S-2 Anantheera Apt, Konnur Gali, B Ward, Mangalwar Peth, Kolhapur -416012. **Phone : 0231 - 2620472.**
Krantivir Tambatkaka Vachanalaya 3 - A Janta Bank Colony, Nana Patil Ring Road, Kolhapur HO, Kolhapur - 416003. **Mobile : +(91) - 8605731771.**	**All Saints Home** 54-A Dockyard Road, Mazagon, 400 010 **Mrs. Sharada Madam - 022-23778357**
Assissi Bhavan C/o Franciscan Hospitaller Sisters of the Immaculate Conception, Near Sai Baba Complex, Goregaon (E), 400063. **Sist. Ubaldine Coelho - 022-28400762**	**F S Parekh Dharmshala** Huges Road, **022-23645982 / 022 22677421**
Little Sisters of the Poor Mahakali Cave Road, Andheri (E), 400 096. **Sist. Mary Joseph - 28382535, 28364187**	**Justice H.K. Chainani Elder's Home** Navghar road, near Shahani estate, Mulund East, Mumbai 400081. **022-25600033**

Rama Narayan Vanaprastha Nivas C/O Shri. P.N. Kulakarni, Phadakwari, V.P.Road, 400 004. Mr. P.N. Kulakarni	Seth Doongarsee Nagji Trust 106/B, Neelam Centre, Hind Cycle Road, Worali, 400 025. Mr. Vasant Thakkar - 020-24923478
Shanti Daan Missionaries of Charity Gorai Creek, Borivali(W), 400 092. Brother Geoff M.C. - 022-28011362	Asha Daan Missionary Charity Society, Near Byculla Fire Brigade, Sankli Road, Byculla, Mumbai - 400027 (022) 23093591
Dr. Desai Hospital A/7 , Ratan Nagar Green way society, Daulatnagar, 10th Road Dahisar post office Borivali (East) 28948806	"Little Sister of the poor" Home for the Aged, (1958) Mahakali Caves Road, Andhreri, Mumbai 400 093 28382535, 28364187
Asha Kiran YWCA Phone No: 91-22-26702831, 26702839, 26702863, 26702872, 26703021	Jeevan Asha Veera Desai Road Andheri (W) 400 058 26236845/26708473
The Society of the Helpers Mary Bal Bhavan-Shraddhha Vihar Veera Desai Road Andheri (W) 400 058 26232546	Cheshire Homes India Bethleham House,Mahakali Road Andheri (East) 28324515
Dr. Dias Nursing Home Shanti sadan 105/7, Perry Road Bandra (West) 400 050 26402283	St. Anthony's Home for the Aged Chapel Road, Bandra (West) 400 050 26424046
Shanti Avedana Ashram (estb.1986) 216, Mount Mary Road, Bandra(Wast)400 050 26427464	Shanti Avedana Ashram 216, Mount Mary Road, Bandra (Wast) 400 050
"Nirmala Niketan" (estb.2/10/1984 Plot No.2, Sector No. 8 , CBD, Belapur, Navi Mumbai 27571555	Missionaries of Charities run "Shantidan" LT Road, Gorai Creek, Boriwali (East) 400 091 28671362/26901362
Emmanuel Health Care Research centre A6/16/4, Jolly Jevan , Boriwali (East)400 091 28075772/28930910	"Shanti Dhan" Home for sick & Dying Destitute Missionaries of Charity Goria Road Boriwali (Wast) 400 092 28671362

"Adhar" OAH (estb.5/4/2000) Daulatnagar, Jain Mandir Road, Behand Hinduja Hall Boriwali (East) Mumbai 400 066 **Phone : 28946463**	Vasant smruti trust's" Kisan Gopal Rajpuria Vanparasthashram" Gorai Village,Near Ramratna vidya mandir, Essel world Road, North gorai Road, Boriwali **Phone: 28450158**
"Ashadan"Missionaries of Charity for dying destitutes. Sakhli Street Byculla, Mumbai 400 008 **Phone : 23093591**	**Shepherd Widow's Home** Shepherd Road Office Clare Road, Byculla Mumbai 400 008 **Phone : 23088726/9819602493**
The Salvation Army Social Service Centre Old Age Home 122 Maulana Azad Road, Byculla Mumbai 400 008 Ph : **022 -23051573 / 223071346**	Jankalyan Sevashram 14 Kusum Chedda Nagar, Chembur 400 089 **Phone : 252 858 16**
Anand Ashram Trust Industry House, Churchgate, Mumbai-400 020 **Phone : 22026340**	**Suman Maternity and Nursing Home** Sahayog Society 1st floor, Gawade Nagar, Near Konkani Dahisar (East) **Phone : 28935754/ 28966731**
"Astitva" Plot No. 8, Phase NO.1 State Bank Road, MIDC, Dombivali (East) 421 203 **Phone : 2471358**	**Shri Gopal OAH** Lokmanya Goshala, Gograswadi Dombivali (East) Thane-421 201 **Phone : 95251-2445684/ 95251-2451076/ 2448810**
Assissi Bhavan Pahadi Estate, Goregoan (Esat) Mumbai-400 063 **Phone : 28400762**	**Kalpataru Vruddashram** 24/259, Shastri Nagar, Goregoan (Wast) Mumbai-400 063
Savitribai Phule Mahil OAH Bhagat Singh Nagar No.1. Goregoan (West) Mumbai-400 104 **Phone : 28792863**	**Durga Maternity and Surgical Home** Chaitanya bungalow, Saraswati baug, Near Rameshwar mandir, Jogeshori (East) 400 060 **Phone : 28325835**
King Geoge Memorial Hospital (193 8) Dr. E. Moses Road after famous Studio, Mahalaxmi Mumbai -400 011 Phone : 24923877	**Our Lady of PietyHome** 49, Vijaywadi J. Shankar Seth Road Marin Line Mumbai- 400 002 **Phone : 22054922**
Setu-Ghar Kamgar Sagam Nirmala Niketan 38 New Marine Lines Pawai Mumbai-400 020 **Phone : 22032615**	**All Saints Home (estb.1897)** 54,A Dockyard Road, Mazgaon, Mumbai- 400 010 **Phone : 23778357**

Strangers Home 155, Motishah Lane, Mazgaon,Mumbai- 400 010	**The Asylum** Case Piedade, Hathi baug, Mazgaon,Mumbai- 400 010 **Phone : 23750319**
F. S. Parekh Dharmashala Darul Muluk, Hugles Road Vasai, Mumbai **Phone : 3645085**	**Jamshetji Jeejibhoy Dharmshala** Shankar Puppala Road, Nagpada Mumbai-400 008 **Phone : 23079838**
Sir Jamshetjii Jeebhoy dharmshala (1947) Jehangir Boman Behram Road, Nagpada Junction, Mumbai-400 008 **Phone : 23051630/23079838**	**Nirala OAH** Neral, Central Railway Neral New Mumbai **Phone : 24301796**
Vanvasi Kalyan Ashram New Palm Beach Housing Society A/5/1/1/Sector -4 Nerul Navi Mumbai **Ph. 022-24113341, 9892268562**	**Matrusadn OAH** Plot No.30 Sector No.10 Phase No. 11, Opp Terna Medical College Nerul Nerul- New Mumbai **Phone : 022-27722360**
"Sharan"OAH (estb.June1997) sector No.9, Near Father Agnel Polytech. Vashi, New Mumbai **Phone : 27654744 / 27659454/55 / 27661849**	**Vatsalya Trust's "Vanprasthashram (estb. 7/2/2000)** Sector 2, Plot No. 11, Sanpada New Mumbai **Phone : 27617390/25782958/25794798**
MBA Foundation's Care Centre for Above 18 MR Adults God's Haven, Crystal palace Complex, Rambaug Area, Near Shriram Ashram Taloja Pawai **Phone : 56003797**	**Dr. Butala, Silver coin Nursing Home** Vakola Pipe line, santacruz (East) Mumbai 400 055 **Phone : 26134774/9869357720**
Cardinal Gracias destiotute's Home Missionaries of Charity, 17, Chapel Lane santacruz (West)Mumbai **Phone : 26492994**	**Mother Teresa's Home** 17 Chapal Lane Santacruz Mumbai(Wast) 400 054 **Phone : 26492994**
Senior Citizen Assistance 10 Shriganesh 18 Linking Road Extn. Santacruz (wast) Mumbai 400 054 **Phone : 26603726**	**Shri Manav seva sangh's "CU Shah** Senior Citizens Home" 255-257, Sion Road, sion (wast) Mumbai-400 022 **Phone : 24015561 / 24092266 / 24071553 / 24077327**
Param Shantidham OAH 15/3/1988 Vairatvasi Abanand Maharaj, Taloja, MIDC Vrudha vadi, Post Vavaje, Near "Techoba" Company, Taloja **Phone : 0731-2695/5927054**	**Navgurga OAH (estb.15/8/1982** Near Aptewadi, Shirgoan, Badlapur, Taluka Ulhasnagar, Thane. **Phone : 25403735**

Swamy Shanti Prakash OAH Main Bazar, camp No 4, OPP section 30 Ulhasnagar ,central Rly Thane **Phone : 2528334**	**Shraddhanand Ashram - Vasai OAH (1966)** Advocate Rajani Marg, Near Deep Mala, zenda Bazar, Vasai Dist-Thane 401 201 **Phone : 24012552/24010715**
Shraddhanand Ashram - Vasai OAH (1927) Advocate Rajani Marg, Near Deep Mala, zenda Bazar, Vasai, Dist-Thane 401 201 **Phone : 95250320124 / 322187 / 24012552 / 24010715**	**Surgical Home** Nityanand Arogyadham, Kankaditya Socity, Sahayog Mandir Road, Ghantali Thane 400 602 **Phone : 25361115**
Dhanwantari OAH(estb.1/2/2000) Patil bldg.Shanti Nagar, Rd., No.27 Wagle Estate Thane **Phone : 25821910**	**Rajpal foundation charitable Hospital** Near Begger Home, Chandansar Road, Virar East Thane **Phone : 95250-503014, 28349250**
"Amrutkrupasgar " Shushrushalay Walivali gaon, Manjarli Road, Badlapur Central Railway, Thane **Phone : 0251-911-691138**	**"Shri Saidham"** Near Khidkaleshwar Mahadeo Mandir, Padlegaon, Thane **Phone : 9820740926**
"Adhar" OAH (estb.7/6/2002) Plot no.6, Chaitraban, Souroli Road, Shahapur,Asangoan Central Railway, Thane	**"Adhar"** Thakurwadi, Mulgaon, Badlapur,Thane **Phone : 5341708**
Manasi Done Road, Post Vangani, Taluka Ambarnath, Thane **Phone : 95251-266-0008**	**Beru Matimand Pratishthan** Taluka Vasai, Thane Thane **Phone : 95251-670589**
"Swayamsiddha" Chinchoti, Near Grampanchayat, Post Kaman, Dhabdhaba Road Taluka Vasai, Thane **Phone : 022-23841326/ 95250-2210372**	**Mr. S.P. Beru Mentally Handicapped Trust (Estb.10/1/1989** Baravi dam Road, Rahtoli, Badlapur (Wast) Central Railway Thane **Phone : 95251-670589 / 95251-673818**
"Adhar" (estb. 1994) Thakurwadi, Mulgaon, Badlapur (West) Central Rail Way ,Thane **Phone : 0251-691476/022-25330895**	**"Niradhar"** 48a, Tokre- Kaner, Taluka Vasai , Virar (East) Thane 401 303 **Phone : 022-24306666/912571110**
Tushar Pawar OAH and Nature cure Centre run by Dr. Keluskar Savara Road, Vangani (Wast) Taluka Ambernath Thane **Phone : 95251-2660039**	**Shanti Niketan Bhagini** Gothivara, Father wadi, Vasai (East) Mumbai-401 205 Vasai

Rajpal Hospital Plot no. 13. sec. No.10. Koparkhairane, New Mumbai- Vashi - 400 709 **Phone : 27549911 / 27549911/27550101**	**Ashraya Elders Paradise** Nerul Road, Sector-19, Nerul(east), Navi Mumbai -400706
Shubham Old Age Care House Mount View Society, Matheran Road, Panvel, Mumbai- 410206 **Phone : 022 - 49431335**	**Ashray Old Age House** 1st Floor, Room No. 723, Rajshree Farm House, Panvel Matheran Road, Panvel, Mumbai- 410206. Land Mark: Near Koproli Village, Panvel. **Phone : 022 - 49430050**
Karuneshwar Old Age Care House Ta 4, Mount View Chs, New Panvel, New Panvel, Panvel, Mumbai- 410206 Land Mark: Near Vihighar Stop, Chilpe Village, Matheran Road, 022 - 49431459 / 9930843395	**Adhar Ghar / Shantivan** Rajeev-Rajan Lad Trust C/o Mr. Vinay V. Ghotge, 301, Adhwar, S. No. 111/9, Prabhat Road, Lane 14, Erandwane, Pune - 411004. **Mr. Vinay Vasant Ghotge: (91)** **9552522132**
Adhar Ghar / Shantivan Shantivan, Nere, New Panvel (10km inside from main old Pune Mumbai Road, Rikhshaw is availble New Panvel 2143238131 / Mr. Vinay **Vasant** **Ghotge: (91) 9552522132**	Sahwaas Dubebaug, Hendre Pada, Badalapur West, 421503 **Rashmi Mate - +91-9892665610** **Miss Deepika C Bhide – +91-** **9833845270** **Mrs. Neema Chinchalkar – +91-** **9730336882 / 7350668489**
Jankalyan Sevashram Plot No. 10 & 11, Mumbai Pune Road, Panvel, Mumbai- 410221 Land Mark: Opposite Canara Bank	Seal Ashram Vangani Village, Nere, Mahalaxmi Nagar, New Panvel, Panvel, Mumbai- 410221 Land Mark: Near Mahalaxmi Nagar **Phone : 022 - 49442841**
Sri Sai Narayan Baba Ashram Plot No. 400/1, Panvel City, Panvel, Mumbai- 410206 Land Mark: Near Panvel Railway Station **Phone : 022 - 7451001**	**My Sweet Home** Shop No. 101/102, Plot No. 42, Shivam Apartment, New Panvel Sector 5/A,New Panvel, Panvel, Mumbai- 410206 Land Mark: Beside Telephone Exchange **Phone : 9594477325**
Consmopolitian Ladies Association Matru Sadan, Phase-II, Sector 10, Plot No. 30, Nerul. **Mrs. Sarala Mehrotre.** 022-27722360	**Narmada Charitable Foundation** Narmada Niketan Home for the Aged, Plot No.2, Sector 8, Near Kokan Bhavan, CBD Belapur, 400 615. **Mr. Ashok bhai : 022-27571555**

Sharan - Kamala Raheja Home for the Senior Citizen Soc. For the Rehabilitation of Parapegic, Plot No.52, Sector 9A, Vashi, 400 703. **Mr. N. L. Nayak** **022-27659454, 27654744, 27661849**	**Swami Vivekanand Charitable Trust** Durgadevi Old Age Home, J-13, Laxmi Nagar, 440 022. **Mr. Shivaji Mohite.** **0712-2225286**
Panchavati Vridha Ashram, Matru Sewa Sangh. Dhighori, Urmer Road, 440 009. **Mrs. Dhanvanti Pandharpurkar** **0712-2711852, 523596**	**Home For Aged & Handicapped** Unthkhana Medical Road Nagpur-440009 **Sr. Irene** **0712-2745091**
Sanjivan Social Medical Foundation Sanjivan Gram Amgao Devli Hingna Road Nagpur **Dr. Sanjay Ugemuge** **M. No.9822470011/9326350459**	**Hemsul Jakate Trust** Umred Road IBP Petrol Pump **Mr. Hemant Jakate** **0712-3944349/9422162646**
Panchavati Vrudhashram Near Bada Tajbagh Umred Road Nagpur **Mrs. Tikekar** **0712-2711852**	**Matoshree Vrudhashram** Adasa Tahsil Saoner Dist. Nagpur **Mr. Kahrade** **2290421/2271303**
Ashvasth Old Age Home Nelco Society Trimurti Nagar **Mrs. Sunanda Patrikar** **0712-2227206/2222590**	**Shanti Bhavan** Katol Road Nagpur -440013 **Phone : 0712-2593080/9866196786**
Pachlegaonkar Vrudhashram Near Narayana Vidyalaya Khapri Nagpur **0712-2275581**	**Maitriban** **Mr. Ravi Gandhe** **0712-2750639**
Prem Dan 250,Mohan Nagar Kingsway Near St. Josephs Girls High School Nagpur -01 **Sr. Priti - 0712-2545544**	**Nirmala Home for the Aged Society** Near H.P.T. Coollege Superior **Phone : 0253-2342047**
Radha Keshav Home for Elders 14-17, Anand Darshan Co-op Society, Near Octrai B, Off Lam Road, Deolal, 422 101. **Mrs. Laxmi Gallani.** **0253-2493494, 09822042043**	**Asmita Charitable Trust, Gunjoti** Indradhanu Vriddha Seva Kendra, Chourasta - Gulbarga Road, N.H.9, Omerga, 413 606. **Dr. Damodar Patange.** **02475-2252004, 2252408, 2252323, 09422069904**

A S R A - Apar Nath Senior Citizens Home Shiva Farm, P.O. Koneregaon Mull Uralikanachan, Pune Solapur Road, 412 202 **Mr. Jaswant Rai Sharma** **0212-2816921, 2816087**	**Anand Ashram** Place-Ranje, Po. Arvi, Tal.Bhor. 412 205 **Mr. S.V. Ranzekar** **020-24221813, 09970021133**
Desai Sahjivan Trust Vanprasthashram, Water Field Compound, Bhangarwadi, Lonavala, Tal.maval, 410 401. **Dr. K.S. Desai.** **020-24327309, 24227281, 24305307, 09820622485**	**Hingane Stree Shikshan Sanstha** **Karve Nagar, 411 052.** **020-2235254**
Home for the Aged Women Maharshee karve Stree Shikshan Sanstha, Karvenagar, 411 052. **Mr. P.L. Deshpande. & Mr. R.L. Deshpande.** **020-22368375, 25431967, 25468975, 25461497**	**Ishaprema Niketan** 972, Nana Peth, Padmaji Park, 411 002. **Mataji Nirmala** **020-22653363,**
Janseva Foundation Late Shri Haribhai V. Desai Old Age Home, Sh Rasiklal Manikchand Dhariwal Old Age, At Post Ambi Ranawadi (Panshet), Tal. Velha, 412107. **Dr. Vinod Shaha &** **Prof. Shinde** **020-24538787, 24538788, 09823011760**	**Jivahala** 19/6, Raikar nagar, Garmal Wadgaon, Dhairi, 411 041. **Dr. Abhyankar** **020-2592012, 24392148**
Matrukul 17, Parvati Payatha, 411 001. **Phone : 020-2543998**	**N.A.B. Lions Home for Aging Blind** Sudhar Baug, Old Khandala Road, Khandala, Tal. Mawal, 410 302. **Ms. Asha Ratnaparkhi.** **02114-273066**
Nivara 96, new Sadashiv Peth, Alka Talkies Marg, Navi Peth, 411 030. **Mrs. Nirmala** **0212-24339918, 2539918**	**Nivrutta Seva Sangh** Vanaprasthashram Plot No 20A; tapodham Vasahat, Talegao (Dabhade) Station, Tal. Mawal, 410 507. **Mr. Ekanath Deshpande.** **020-24434511, 02114-225768**
Pariwar Mahila Niwas Ganesh Mala, Withalwadi Road. **Dr. Shailja Rajwade**	**Poona Diocesan Corporation (PDC)** 410/11, Nanapeth, 411 002. **Sister Amaln- 020-651337**

Poona Widows Home **3, Solapur Road, 411 001.** **Sister Ursula F.S.-** **020-2663389**	**Pune Mahila Mandal** 17, Parvati Payatha, 411 009. **Mrs. Manda Shimpi** **020-24443548**
Sandhya Home for the Aged 410/11, Nanapeth, 411 002. **Sister of St. John The Baptist** **020-2651337**	**Savali Vrudhashram** Plot No.32, Maskerness Colony, Opp. Atemplast Factory, Talegaon Dhamadhere, 412 208. **Mrs. Chanada Amdekar** **02114-22792**
apla ghar khanapur, pune **phalnikar - 9850227077**	**Anandadham** At. Jambhulpada, Tal- Sudhagad, 410 205 **Mr. V.S. Palekar - 0952142-2244104,** **2244089**
Kushtrog Nivaran samiti Ramkrishna Niketan Vridhashram, Shantivan, Tal. Panvel, 410 206. **Mr. Govind Shinde** **952143-2238070, 2238153, 2238331**	**Nisargopachar Health Resort &** **Nirala Vridhashram** **Dr. Pal's Nirala, Neral, 410 101.** **022-24300780, 24300885**
Paramshanti Dham Vriddhashram **Trust** Taloja MIDC, Near Technova Co., Post Koyanavele, Tal.Panvel, 410 208. **Mahant Abanandgiri Maharaj** **022-27412695, 27863544, 09423032049**	**Ramadham Vridhashram, Adoshi** **Village** Khopoli-Pen Road, Shilpatha, Khopoli Taluka, Khalapur, 410 203. **Mr. Subir Kumar Choudhaary** **022-26656224, 26662133, 26655644.**
Bhagirathi Vridhashram Nalavade, Po.Karjuve, Tal. Sangeshwar, 415 608. **Mr. Govind Tukaram**	**Pathak Trust's Vruddhashram,** Garde Wada, Opp. Old Murlidhar Temple, Brahminpuri, Miraj, 416 410. **Dr. R.N. Pathak - 223252, 222652**
Matoshree Vridhashram A/Po. Gopalpur, Tal. Pandharpur, 413 304. **Mr. bhagavanrao Patil.** **02428-2248035, 0982274309**	**Papa Hospital for Aged Sick** Shanti Nagar, Road No.27, Wagle Industrial Estate, 400 604. **Phone : 4300885, 5323088**
Shraddhanand Mahilashram Vasai OAH.(estb 1927). Adv. Rajani Marg, Near Deep mala, Zenda bazaar,Vasai, District Thane 401201	**Shraddhanand Mahilashram,** Shraddhanand Marg, Maheshwari udyan, Matunga, Mumbai 400019. **Phone : 95250 320124 / 322187** **24012552/24010715**

Old Age Home Run By Institute of Public Assistance (Provedoria) Mala, Panaji, Goa.

Name of Old Age Home	Place	Tel. No.
Recelhimento de Serra,	Althino Panaji	2220982
Asylum of Chimbel	Chimbel	2443856
Asylum of Mapusa	Mapusa	2256238
Asylum of Candolim	Candolim	2489935
Asylim of Majorda	Majorda, Salcete	2791362
Asylim of Loutolim	Loutolim	2858514
Asylim of Margoa	Margao	2713294
Centro de Cunculim	Cunculim, Salcete	2866383
Centro de Chinchinim	Chinchinim, Salcete	2864199

OLD AGE HOMES RUN BY CATHOLIC MISSIONS		
Name of Old Age Home	Place	Tel. No.
Ark of Hope (St. Vincent de Paul Society)	Candolim	2489918
Asilo "Dr. Rafael Pereira"	Benaulim	2770210
Asyium of the Sacred Heart of Jesus and Mary	Aldona	2293195
Bom Jesus Home	Nachinola	2293319
Clergy Home	Porvorim	2417318
Clergy Home	Margao	2706259 / 2715146
Divine Providence Home	Benaulim	2788945 /09890917570 (Sr Mary John) / 08390588270 (Sr Pauline F'des)
Holy Family Home for Aged	Chora	2239239
Holy Spirit Home	Moira	2470216
Home for the Aged (St. Vincent de Paul Society)	Vasco Da Gama	
Isha Prem Niketan	Goa-Velha	2218507
Isha Prem Niketan	Assagao	2268913
Krist Raj Bhavan	Saligao	2278345

Lar Santa Margarida	Divar	2280465 / 2280050
Mae de Deus Home	Saligaon	2278361
Mother Marry Haven	Calangute	2276278
Nazareth Home	Navelim	2711004
Our Lady Of Perpetual Succour (Home for the Aged)	Sonarbhat, Guirim	6454911
St. John of God's Home	Old-Goa	2285742
St. Joseph's Asylum	Cobravaddo, Calangute	2281013
St. Joseph's Eventide Home	Ucassaim	2261528
St. Joseph's Home	Siolim	2270731
St. Mary's Guest House	Nagoa, Verna	2278332
St. Mary's Home	Siolim	2272334
St. Thomas Villa	Bodiem	2298507
Missionaries of Charity	Karmali	
Missionaries of Charity	Panaji	
Dr. Alferd Home	Chandor	
St. Judes Helpling Hand Home	St. Estevam	

OTHER OLD AGE HOMES		
Name Of Old Age Home	Place	Tel. No.
"Sneha Mandir"	Bandora, Ponda	2335548
"Sanjeevan"	Bandora, Ponda	2335257
Vijaya Ashram	Vovonem,Tivim	6512456
Our Home	Vasco	2538329
Three Roses Mother Teresa Ashram	Colvale	
Mahilashram	Muddi	2912015
Vishwanath Jagannath Trust	Ponda	
Padusai (Mrs. Sarika Pednekar)	Moira	9011838594
Mr. Joe D'sa	Mapusa	

About the Author

Name:	**Dr. Anil Gandhi**
DoB:	13 August 1939, Madha, Solapur, Maharashtra
Education:	M.B.B.S. (1963), M.S., B.J. Medical College (1971)

Five years practice in Pune as Family Physician

Rural Medical Service in villages in Pune district 1966 -1986

Gandhi Hospital established in 1970

Completed specialization in Colorectal Surgery From St. Marks' Hospital, London (1974)

Presented several research papers in International Conferences up to 1984

Honorary professor at B.J. Medical College, Tilak Ayurved Mahavidyalay, Bharati Vidyapeeth, Dhondumama Sathe Homeopathy College. Honorary Surgeon at Kamala Nehru Hospital, Pune.

Social work: Started work related to hygiene, education and Development in the adivasi area of Pangloli, Lonavla Also started an ashram school which is running successfully. Participation in the national initiative of national integration by Purvseema Vikas PratishthanPresident, Maharashtra Technical Education Society, Pune

Publications: **Mana Srujana** Autobiography in Marathi, three editions sold in just five months. Received first prize from Marathi Wangmay Parishad, Baroda. Articles appreciating Mana Srujana published in many leading newspapers and

literary periodicals Mana Srujana translated
and published in Gujarathi (Ahmedabad),
English (Mumbai), Hindi (Delhi)

A series of articles published for three months in
Maharashtra Times, called 'Sagun-Nirgun' Articles
published in Sakal, Saptahik Sakal, Loksatta
Edited and compiled

Dhanwantari Gharoghari in August 2011

Wichari Mana published in June 2013

Shodh Manacha, collection
of short stories, 2013

High Tech Life Line, March 2014

Brain, The Master, November 2015

Sanjeevani Ucch Tantradnyanachi, June 2015

Aflatuun Mendu, May ,2016

Dev Danwa Nare

Nirmile : About to be published **Ya Katerweli... Ananadi Wrudhatwakade Watchal,**

Jeevansandhya... Khushahal Vrudhavasta ki aur and **Twilight of Life... Helpful Hints for Ageing Gracefully,** to be published in October 2016, on the occasion of World Elder Day

Public Lectures: Lecture in Wasant Wyakhyan Mala Pune on
26 April 2011 on the subject 'Family Doctor'

Lecture in Wasant Wyakhyan Mala, Wai on
2 May, 2011 on the subject 'Experiences
in the Medical Profession'

20, Laxmi Society, Senapati Bapat Marg,
Pune 16. Phone no. 020-24459930 / 25653000
Mobile: 9422009466

Help-Age India

HelpAge, India arranges a number of activities for the aged.
Seniors participating in various sporting events

Homes built by HelpAge, India for
tsunami affected people

Citizens participating in mobile healthcare services rendered
by HelpAge Indiain cities and villages

Mr. Matthew Cherian (CEO) HelpAge India, receiving,
'Wayoshreshth' award at the hands of Hon. Governor

Janseva Foundation

Senior citizens chit chatting comfortably in the Home

Old Home with Modern amenities

Senior Citizens at Janseva Foundation Old Home

Officers' visit to Shri Rasiklal Manikchand Dhadiwal
Old Home

Athashri Foundation

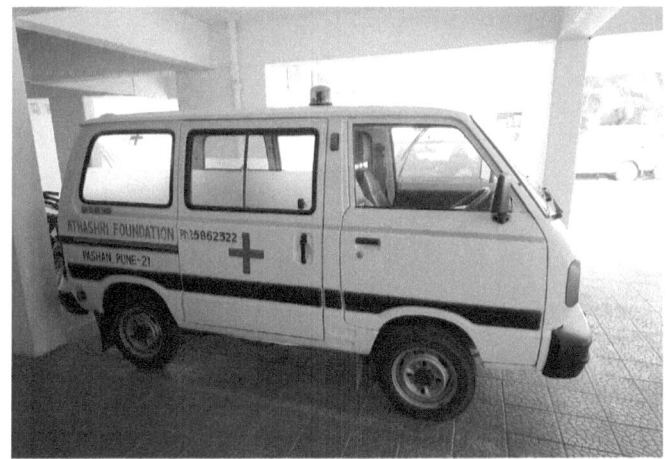

Ambulance facilities available 24/7

Wide spread Athashri facility for the old with Modern
equipments

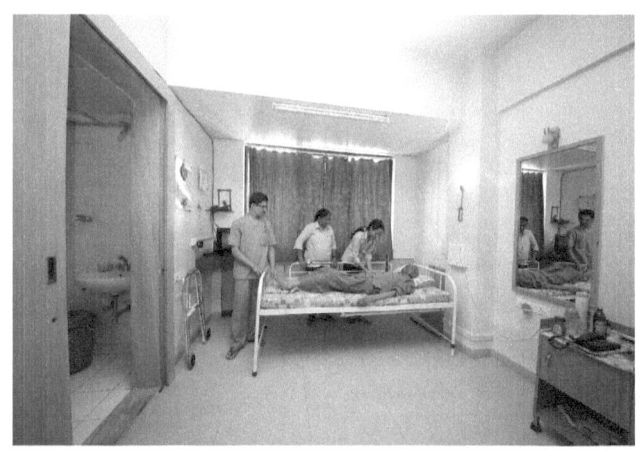

The modern kitchen that caters to the taste buds of the elders in the Home

Minivan for elders to move about the Old Home campus

State- of –the- art Gym

The extensive Athashri Campus in its greenery

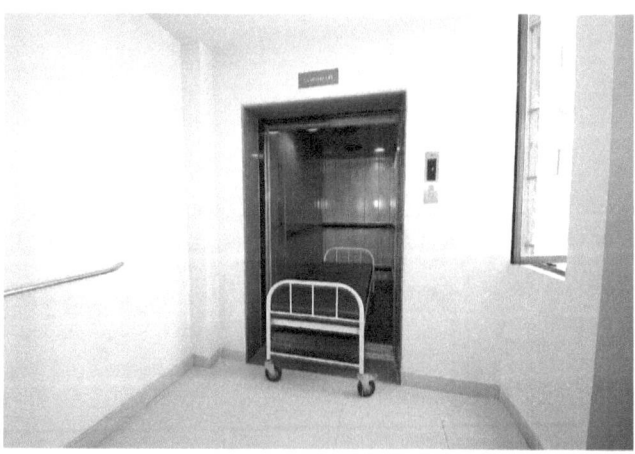

Convenient lifts in the building, which can accommodate
stretchers for sick elders

www.ingramcontent.com/pod-product-compliance
Lightning Source LLC
Chambersburg PA
CBHW030322020726
47493CB00004B/1132